SUPERHERO CYBERPUNK ADVENTURE

I0672354

SHADOW DRAGON 3:
THE FALL
OF CERES

WADE COLEMAN

1

Shadow

Dragon 3

Wade Coleman

October 2023 Edition

TABLE OF CONTENTS

PART ONE – THE NIGHT WE MET

PART TWO – THE FALL OF CERES

PART THREE – RESTORATION

Foreword

I love writing fiction. I leave this world for a few hours daily and enter one of my creations. I race to finish the first draft of my novels. It's like the Anna Nalick lyrics, "If I get it all down on paper, it's no longer inside of me, threatening the life it belongs to."

After the first draft, the fun starts by filling in dialogue and details that bring the world to life. When I'm in the zone, the characters write their own dialogue. I used a three-ring binder and pen to write this novel's ideas and plot points. Then, I wrote the scene without consciously knowing where I was headed. I found this looser outline style a bitter fit for my personality.

When writing a scene, I use music to get me in the mood. Music is my muse. There is nothing like listening to creative people to get the creativity flowing. However, I rarely listen to music when I write. I prefer silence to hear the music and dialogue in my head.

It was a lot of fun creating the Natasha and Hermes relationship. Hermes can't hide anything from Natasha. And so he was forced into being honest. I found it fun to write in juxtaposition to all the other women in Hermes' life.

Part One

The Night We Met

Chapter One

I check out my pecs in a full-length mirror. I'm disappointed. I was hoping I'd be more buff.

Natasha stands beside me, wearing a sandy brown pantsuit matching her hair. Natasha is my implant. She's an artificial intelligence that controls most of my central nervous system and brain stem. Natasha is intimately integrated into my nervous system and can project any sense into my brain except smell. Only I can see her. Knowing this, Natasha tends to limit her appearances to when I am alone. However, even in company, her 'voice' communicates everything she wants me to know. It was initially challenging, but I've gotten used to her frequent interruptions.

"I'm fat," I say, pinching my belly. "Look, that's almost an inch. I used to have six-pack abs, and now I'm down to a four-pack. In a few years, I'll have a gut like Daniel."

"Darling, I have known you for two years, and you've never had a six-pack."

I let out a sigh. "You're not just saying that to make me feel better?"

A few weeks ago, my muscle and bone augmentations were completed. They added three pounds of bone and ten pounds of muscle. I can't see any difference in the mirror, but they make me stronger. Now, I can climb a rope without using my legs. When you've got assassins on your tail, I suppose function should be more important than beauty.

I turn 90-degrees and glare at my butt. "It disappears when I turn sideways."

Natasha pats my ass. "You have a runner's butt."

I blush and get dressed. Natasha knows how to make me feel better.

I recently turned 27, and I've already got grey hair. It's probably stress. I had to sell Frisco Nights because the Baron doesn't play fair. He sent assassins to target my actors and staff. Being a man of leisure doesn't suit me. I was so bored I played bingo with my mom at church. I shudder at the memory, then head downstairs to make coffee and breakfast.

Last year, a group of bandits planned an attack on Ceres. We caught them in time, but Baron realized I was a walking bag of tricks. He probably hired an intelligence firm to ascertain my vulnerabilities and kill me if they could. Now, Ceres is my prison.

I finish breakfast, clean up, and take my coffee outside. I use my foot to push the button that opens the doors. The original sliding glass door was a security threat. It was replaced with six nickel, steel, and ceramic laminate doors, one capping the outside and three feet behind it and the other standing flush against the inside wall.

It's May; the air is crisp and fragrant with tree blossom. In the last eighteen months, I rebuilt the raised beds and greenhouse. The four-foot-wide, eight-foot-long beds form a nested rectangle in my backyard. The plastic pipe greenhouse has been replaced; the new one has a metal frame around translucent plexiglass.

Coffee in hand, I walk around the front yard. There's a circular driveway,

12

a freestanding hemp and plastic bale three-bay garage directly opposite my house, and a second, smaller garage is attached to the right side of the house.

One of Bob's roosters scratches and pecks under an orange tree. He picks up a dead snake in his beak, looks at me, and runs away with his prize.

"What? You think I want some of that?"

"Natasha, I'm calling in a favor," I say.

She appears next to me, wearing a fur-lined coat and boots that match her hair. "What is it?"

"We're going to Vegas."

"Do you think he'll let us?"

"If he doesn't, his new name is Colonel Liar, Liar, Pants on Fire."

Chapter Two

I'm inside Café Americain, sitting on a barstool with tassels, when Bogart comes over and pours me a bourbon.

A young girl climbs onto the stool next to me. She's in black and white, except for a mop of curly red hair. She looks like Shirley Temple.

"Rick, I'll have a Shirley Temple," she says, then looks at me. "Mom thinks I'm evil."

"You're not evil. You have to test the limits by pushing past them. That way, you know where the limit is."

"You get me," the girl says.

"You have the Conrad gene. So, it would be best to go free-range until you

*turn seven. By then, you'll be settled
enough for school."*

*"I'll drink to that," she says, and
we clink glasses.*

* * *

I wake with a smile. Today,
Natasha and I are going to Las Vegas.
I'll be Rick Savage from Denver. I rented
the jet under that name, an F16 with a
laser cannon and missiles. It costs
50,000 credits an hour to fly. Firing a
rocket will cost me a quarter of a million
if needed.

An F16 has no room for luggage,
so my clothes were shipped a week ago
and await my arrival at Caesars Palace.
Nothing is too good for my alter-ego,
Rick Savage.

I wear jeans, a button shirt,
cowboy boots and a hat. Natasha is

wearing a matching outfit, except for her shoes and hat, which are sandy blonde like her hair.

"You look great," I say.

Natasha nibbles on my ear, and my heart skips a beat. I know she's just a mental projection, but she is very cute.

"It's been over a year since we had sex," Natasha says.

I nod vigorously. "I know. It's not my fault the Baron is trying to kill me, and I'm stuck in Ceres, where everyone knows me."

Natasha pats my ass. "Actually, it is your fault. You need to take responsibility for your actions."

"You mean saving Frisco from the bad guys."

"Exactly, we're heroes, the good guys."

"I'm confused; what is your point?"

"The point is we're horny. Everything will make sense after we get laid."

Natasha has replaced the primitive part of my brain that experiences fear, anger and arousal. Since she went rogue, she's become a separate personality with her desires, which are often sexual. She wants me to get a steady girlfriend, but I've burned too many bridges in this small town.

Instead of making breakfast, I drive to Maggie's Diner. Over the last year, the population of Ceres has doubled again from 1,540 to 3,300. When the Broadmoor burned, many retired Navy took their insurance money and moved to Ceres.

During the virus riots, my father, Daniel, and his old war buddies raided a bonded warehouse. Inside was a 1925 Rolls-Royce Phantom. It took Daniel a year to find a buyer. He refuses to tell me how much he got for it.

The next day, Colonel Baker went on a buying spree. Within six months, Ceres had paved roads and sixty new homes. After the construction, thousands of genetically engineered cherry trees were planted by school kids. Our class planted our fair share of the blackberry vines that line the perimeter fence.

Maggie's is on the corner of Main and Baker Street. I take the last open parking spot out front. I leave my cowboy hat on the seat and walk inside. The diner has booths lining the walls and tables in the center. In the back is a counter where farmers occupy half the stools: ex-military men wearing army surplus boots, jeans, and khaki green t-shirts. The navy blue brigade takes the booths. I walk to the back and sit on a stool.

An elf with black hair and blue skin pours me coffee and takes my order.

Someone sits next to me, and I turn to look. "Vike, why aren't you in school?"

"I'm doing a story on you for the school paper."

Vike is psychic, so she knows exactly when and where to show up.

"No comment," I say.

Vike frowns and opens her big violet eyes. "Come on, everyone around here is boring."

"Okay, what do you want?"

"How did you get a nine-foot croc into the Baker High School pool?"

I chuckle, then say, "No comment. But hypothetically speaking, you might need a troll's help."

Vike types on her tablet. "How did you steal a whole warehouse full of rice."

"It wasn't a warehouse; it was alleged that a classroom used for storage was found empty. But, hypothetically speaking, I would steal it one bag at a time."

Vike types some more, and my food arrives. She waits for me to take a bite of the omelet to ask her next question. "Are you pure evil?" She smirks.

After swallowing, I say, "Only on Halloween. I think this year I'll do a haunted house."

"You should do a haunted house," she says and types more. "That will be my headline. Hermes is sponsoring Baker High School's haunted house."

Before I can protest, she slips away, so I finish my breakfast. My phone beeps, and the autopilot on the F16 tells me it's ten minutes out.

I pay with a silver dime and leave a second one as a tip. The elf server gives me a wink. I get in the truck, back out, and continue along Main Street until the intersection. To the east is the Sacramento Estuary and a newly paved road. On the right is a sign to Green Acres. It's the new troll subdivision. Somcone spray-painted: 'is a place to be.' Trolls like TV shows where nobody gets hurt and everybody laughs.

We pass through the first set of hills, then take a right to the airport. It's in a strong defensive position with coastal mountains to the left and foothills to the right.

I travel a few hundred yards and take another right into a newly paved parking lot. Daniel's and Colonel James' trucks are already there, and I pull up next to them. They want to see the F16 up close. They're standing outside in the building's shade. I take my hat and join them. I look at my phone to track the F16's arrival.

"Let me see that," Colonel James says, taking my phone. He looks at the screen. "Two minutes."

I put up with Colonel James because he's the Mayor and the base commander of Ceres. Since first grade, I've called him Colonel James instead of Baker's last name. Sometimes, it's a term of endearment; normally, I'm just being cocky.

Major Hayes pulls in and walks over next to us.

Soon, we hear the roar of a jet engine as the F16 banks to our right and lines up with the runway. After taxiing to the end of the runway, it shuts down. A fueling robot parks close and fills the tank.

We stroll over to inspect the fighter. It's fifty feet long. The four of us walk under the wings and check the missiles. Two are mounted on each side.

"This F16 can electrify the fuselage and create a plasma around the jet that makes it invisible to radar and lets the fighter cruise at Mach 2. Naturally, the jet's radar doesn't work while in stealth mode," I say, going full geek.

The trio nods approvingly.

Daniel walks over to the front. "Where's the cannon?"

I point to a black half-sphere mounted on the nose cone. "That's a one-megawatt laser cannon."

"Nice," Daniel says.

"The artificial intelligence installed in the F16 is a decorated combat veteran. I feel safe."

"Don't underestimate Baron," the Colonel says. "He hates you, Hermes, more than he hates me."

The fuel tanker rolls away, and a box with wheels rolls over to the jet and unfolds into steps. It's a versatile robot that can be reassembled into a ramp, forklift, or steps.

"Who is Hermes," I say, putting on my hat. "I'm Rick Savage."

We laugh. I climb the stairs and get in the cockpit. The cowling slides closed. The two engines rev up, and I wave goodbye.

While the F16 taxies, Natasha and the AIs talk shop. I feel like a third wheel. I rented the fighter jet. You would think I'd get some stick time, but only Natasha gets to drive. I would complain, but it's Natasha's vacation, too, and I have already promised not to whine for the whole week.

Rick Savage has half a million credits to spend over seven days. I'll have to pace myself.

I relax into the cockpit and notice there is not much elbow room. We're five hundred miles from Vegas, and I quickly realize it's a bad idea to bring a cowboy hat into a cockpit. After a few minutes, we break the sound barrier. It's a lot quieter in the cabin when you outrun the engine's noise. Stealth mode engages, and the jet's surface emits a soft blue glow. Soon, we are cruising at

1,200 miles per hour, and it isn't long before we're on approach for landing.

After Natasha smooth talks Las Vegas air traffic control, we are promoted to next in line. She puts all three wheels down simultaneously, and we taxi to a private hanger. The engines power down, and a tug pulls us inside. The cowling opens, and stairs roll up to the cockpit.

I grab my hat and get into character. Rick Savage is from Denver and manufactures textile equipment. I go through a private screening and find my way to arrivals. I wait a few minutes for my ride to show up. It's a standard Vegas strip limo. Rick is a flashy guy. The limo stops, and an amply buxom woman opens my door. I smile big and get in.

Inside, there's a mug of coffee and chocolate. The limo rolls forward, and the chauffeuse asks, "Where we headed?"

"Well, ma'am, I was gonna say Caesars Palace, but first, I need some real coffee. Something with more caffeine. This weak-ass milk chocolate will not do."

"I know a place." She smiles into the rearview mirror. "Mr. Savage, you want music?"

"It's Rick, Cowboy Rick. *Betty Davis Eyes*, Kim Karnes, the extended mix version." I love that song. I like how Kim sings *Betty Davis eyesssss*.

The sunsets and cold creeps over my skin, improving my good mood. Finally, my driver approaches a coffee shop and opens the door. I give her a hundred credit bill and send her in for coffee and chocolate while listening to Kim Carnes. No one sings letter S like Kim Carnes.

27

Vegas is an open-carry town; more than half of the people we pass have pistols, and the rest probably concealed them. Las Vegas cultivates the Wild West style. Buildings are limited to three stories, and the walkways are wood. All the men wear hats, and the women have glitzy clips and feathers in their hair.

"My chauffeusssse, instead of heading straight to the hotel, how about we cruise?"

"It's Kelly, and what are ya looking for? Sightseeing or something specific?"

"Am I asking too much? For little of that human touch?"

"I know a place," she says.

"I'm not looking for a place. I want someone to spend the night cruising in a limo and then the wee morning hours between the sheets."

We stop at a light, and a couple crosses the street. The man wears a black leather jacket down to his knees. I must have one.

Kelly's talking on the phone. "Yeah, he's your type." A pause. "He's cute and wearing designer everything." Another pause. "Okay, bye."

We cruise the strip and pass Caesars Palace. Like everything on the strip, it's lit by LEDs. With my shadow-shifting skills, this is my playground. I definitely need to steal something.

Since I turned thirteen, I've been able to step into a shadow and step out the other side. It's not magic. You dissemble your body into the cold, dark void of nothing, and a few seconds later, it's reassembled on the other end of the shadow. It was terrifying the first dozen times, but now I have a completely different perspective on bodies and solid matter. It doesn't bother me anymore.

We pull into a convenience store beside a mutant with large round eyes and more than ample everything else. She's wearing a leather skirt that barely covers her butt and a matching V-neck blouse, bonnet, and purse. Kelly opens the door for the woman, who spits a wad of gum, gets in and sits close.

"You like to dance?" she asks.

"I like to dance, but I desperately need a leather jacket before we do."

She pats my thigh. "I know a place."

Chapter Three

I'm standing under a black and white neon sign, Rick's Café Americain. I walk inside and sit beside the red-headed girl, drinking a Shirley Temple.

Bogart pours me a bourbon, and I slam three in a row.

"Mom loves you but is not in love with you," Shirley says.

"I loved your mom thc first timc I laid eyes on her," I reply.

*   *   *

I wake to fingers being run through my hair. I smile and open my eyes. It's Natasha.

"Darling, I can't thank you enough for last night."

Clamiady Jane was fun company. She knew all the underground clubs, music and dance scenes. I'm not sure if she's a prostitute. However, I spent 1,500 credits on leather outfits. And 200 credits when she went to the bathroom, but I assume that's for drugs. Ms. Jane gave me her phone number.

I check the clock— 5 PM. I get out of bed, shower, and get dressed. Natasha convinces me to wear my new leather jacket, which reaches my knees, with a steampunk hat and goggles. I exchange the fashion goggles for my night vision ones. It's good to be prepared for anything. Natasha approves of the new leather; she thinks the buttons are very distinguished. I like the surplus of pockets. The Flubber boots are made of a springy material that returns ninety-five percent of your step's force. I walk out of my room with a bounce to my step.

I kill time by checking out the pool and lobby. The hotel has gold gilding on the columns and beams. The promenade is filled with shops that sell expensive watches and jewelry. I lose track of time in the Roman armor exhibit, and Natasha reminds me of our reservation.

A woman in a toga takes me to a seat by the fireplace. I order vodka and relax in a comfy chair. And there she is, sitting in a booth with a man. Pam was my surgical nurse during my face augmentation and cleaned up my dead nervous system after Natasha replaced it. Unfortunately, I had one date with her and screwed up big time. She's wearing the necklace I gave her. An eight-carat heart-shaped ruby in a gold setting and chain, cut from the ten-carat ruby I pried out of the eye of the Kukan Dragon and crafted into a heart shape to disguise its origin. The man she's with has a mustache, so he's obviously a villain.

Pam notices me staring, and our eyes lock. Soon, the waitress delivers a vodka martini and says it from Pam.

I take my drink to her table. The man has rugged good looks that I envy.

"What gave me away?" I ask.

"It's your cock-of-the-walk swagger and Jack Nicholson grin," Pam says smugly.

I sip my martini while trying to come up with something clever and witty, but I get nothing.

"Please sit down," the man says. "Carlos, this is...."

"Rick Savage," I say, and we shake hands.

"How do you know each other?" Carlos asks.

I want to lie, but can't take my eyes off Pam. She's wearing a black cocktail dress with a tantalizing V-shaped décolletage. Her hair is shoulder length and black with red roots.

Another round of drinks while we chat. Even more drinks after.

"I don't mean to pry. Do you two have history?"

Pam takes a sip and looks at me.

"We had one date, maybe two," I say. "Like usual, I screwed up, and she dumped me. Those fancy socialite customs are too complicated for a simple country boy."

"What happened?"

"Apparently, a near-death experience on the first date is a faux pas."

Carlos looks at Pam. She nods.

I raise my hands and give my practiced dumb-ass expression. "Who knew?"

We laugh. Pam snorts but is too tipsy to care.

"That and men like you," I say, then finish my drink.

"Go on," Carlos says.

"Pam has a type," I say, looking at her. "Tall, dark, handsome, charming, honest, non-sociopaths." I raise my hands. "Impossible standards."

We laugh, and Carlos's phone beeps. He checks his message and grins.

"Excuse me, but my wife is expecting me, and I have other duties to attend to." Carlos gets up and kisses

36

Pam's hand. "Thank you so much, Pamela, mother of my child."

Pam smiles at him in a way that makes my heart ache. I feel a twinge of envy as Carlos walks away.

An awkward silence descends.

"You look great," I say to break it.

"I know," Pam says. "I'm wearing an interactive dress designed to keep my shape exactly the right proportions."

"The designer deserves a Nobel Prize," I reply.

"Come on." She grabs my hand. "I want to show off my dress; let's gamble."

I stand up. "Well, if you insist."

Instinctively, I find the craps tables. I invariably win at dice games, Monopoly, and Risk—naturally lucky, except in love.

I wait for the come-out roll, and the stickman hands me the dice. I put a yellow one-thousand-credits chip on eleven.

"Seven, seven, come eleven," I say, rolling the dice.

"Yo-leven, front-line winner," the pit woman says.

I let my bet ride, and others make their bets. Then I say the magic words, "Seven, seven, come eleven."

"Yo-leven," the pit woman says, passing out the fifteen-to-one odds on my bet. The dealer place three flags near my yellow chip.

I roll three more elevens before a giant hand grabs my shoulder and picks me up. It's a troll. He tucks me under one arm, Pam under the other, and strides to a bank of elevators.

"Hey, where's my fifty million?"

"Rick, don't antagonize him, please," Pam says.

We enter a troll-sized elevator and rise two floors. It opens into a Roman bathhouse gilded in gold. A dozen women—trolls, elves, dwarves, and humans—are lounging about. Others sit on chairs with phones or tablet computers.

A troll sits beside a hot tub in a gilded chair, a five-pint glass of beer in his huge hand. We're conveyed toward him. I'm all smiles, waving at the ladies like I'm a celebrity rather than a prisoner. Pam is lowered gently to her feet while I'm unceremoniously dropped on all fours. The troll is wearing shorts, flip-flops, and a gold chain with 'Mr. Big' in sparkling letters. The necklace must weigh a few pounds.

"Strip," Mr. Big says. His smile reveals freshly sharpened teeth.

Never resisting an opportunity to be the center of attention, I remove my clothes sexily.

"Do you want help?" he asks Pam.

Pam takes off her clothes. We hang them on hooks and then stand naked in front of the troll and his entourage.

A man dressed like security in a black suit and sunglasses walks over, carrying a plastic bin.

"Did you find any gadgets to rig a craps table?"

"Well, Mister Big, I don't know what to make of it all." He lays my belongings on a nearby bench. "Med Kit, three disposable phones, five penlights, a set of skeleton keys, a *Covert Companion* lockpick set, and three cans of silly string, two of which are empty."

I smile. The silly string was from last night's rave. Everyone stares at me. Pam pinches her eyebrows together.

Mr. Big glares. "How did you roll five elevens in a row?"

I shrug. "I'm lucky."

"Really? We'll soon discover your secret. Find Drew." Mr. Big lowers himself into the water and motions for us to follow.

A few women join us, the rest watch, only a couple feign disinterest.

"I'm Rick Savage. Pleased to meet you."

"I'm Pam." She puts her hand out to exchange handshakes.

Mr. Big glances at Pam's hand, then redirects his eyes to her mesmerizing tits bobbing in the water.

He picks up my lockpick set. "So, are you working?"

"I'm on vacation. That's just in case of emergencies."

"What kind of emergencies?"

"I'm a consultant," I say, moving my hands. "People lose things, and I find them for a fee. I'm ready if someone needs something found while I'm on vacation."

He picks up my med kit. "I see you like to play doctor. I presume that's just in case, too."

"Shit happens," I say.

"Who's the redhead?"

"Some chick I met in the bar." It's good that lying comes easy to me or that one might make me blush; if I'm in trouble, the last thing I want is to drag Pam down with me.

"If you're on vacation, why bring all the tools of your trade?"

"I like to be prepared."

"Like a boy scout," a dark blue elf with violet eyes says.

Pam bursts out laughing, then stops abruptly. "Sorry, I'm a little nervous."

Mr. Big looks at the elf. "Drucilla, what do you think?"

"He's full of shit. One thing's for sure, he's a practiced liar."

"Give him the taste test," Mr. Big says.

The plump, dark elf wades over and gives me a sniff. She waves her forked tongue at me before licking my cheek. "Yuck!" She spits into the hot tub, grabs a towel, and scrubs her tongue.

"Are you okay?" Mr. Big asks.

She points at me. "That's a sigma six."

"Really?" Mr. Big's eyes widen.

43

"Oh yeah. That's the most bitter thing I've ever tasted. He's a sigma six."

Mr. Big's smile is wide. "I can see by the puzzled expression you don't know what a sigma six is. As a mutant, you're six standard deviations away from normal. That's a one-in-five-hundred-million chance.

"There aren't that many mutants on the planet," Drucilla says.

Everyone scowls at me, even Pam.

"Sorry, I was born," I say.

Mr. Big laughs, and everyone joins in. He studies me for a few minutes when the laughter dies down. "What do you think?"

"I can't read him with smell, taste, or touch. My eyes say he's telling the truth, but my gut doesn't trust him. I need to hear him sing."

Mr. Big smiles. "Do you know a catchy tune?"

I like dealing with trolls. They hate violence and always look for nonviolent resolutions. "If you want to hear me sing, I'll need a piano or keyboard and a place with good acoustics."

"The sigma six is a showman," Mr. Big says, clapping his hands.

Of course, Mr. Big has a piano room. I'm taken backstage to a room with a gold star on the door. Natasha stands behind me, wearing a black velvet cocktail dress with a straight-neck sand-blonde hair skimming her shoulders.

"I don't know which song to sing?"

"Yes, you do," Natasha says.

"Billy Joel? Noooo. It doesn't have a beat."

"It's your best song."

When I had my vocal cords and voice box augmented, I requested the range of Eddie Vedder, but the doctor told me my hardware was all wrong. I'm a tenor.

There's a knock on the door, and it opens.

"You're up," Drucilla says.

She leads me around the corner to a piano and stool. I sit down and look at the audience. A spotlight casts a bright circle around me, obscuring my view. It isn't long before my cyber-eyes adjust. Mr. Big is in a bar with tables and chairs at the back. Pam is center stage, and the girls from the bathhouse sit close by.

Natasha controls my hands and plays the opening riff. I'm nervous, so I close my eyes. "She's got a way about her," I sing. Initially self-conscious, I quickly settle down and lose myself in the lyrics.

When I dare to open my eyes, I look at Pam. "She's got a smile that heals me." I close my eyes again and let the music and lyrics flow through me. Then Natasha stops playing, and I look up.

Pam brushes away a tear. The bathing beauties clap and whistle. When the applause stops, all eyes turn to Mr. Big. He looks at Drucilla.

"I still can't read much, but he loves the redhead."

"Well, duh," Mr. Big says and laughs. "I got something for ya. It's right up your alley."

Chapter Four

Pam and I are in a hotel room with no windows. The only exit is guarded by two men. When I check through the peephole, I can see their silhouettes, so I know they're still there. It's a comfortable prison with a king-sized bed, mini-fridge, couch and coffee table.

It's one o'clock, so Pam and I sleep in bed. At least she sleeps. I keep looking at my virtual watch.

At 5 AM, I wake bleary-eyed after less than an hour of sleep. I can't remember the last time I was up this early. The girl of my dreams lies a few inches away from me. It is technically our second date, and has gone much better than the first. Pam rolls over, and her arm snakes around my waist. I hold her hand and doze.

"Hermes," Pam whispers into my ear. "Can I have my hand back?"

I face her, wrap my arm around her waist, and pull her close. "Is it okay if I hold you?"

Pam replies with a kiss.

*   *   *

The door opens around four in the afternoon, and Drucilla enters with a guy in a black suit and wraparound sunglasses.

"Mr. Big is ready for you." Then she points to Pam. "You can stay here."

49

We return to the piano room. I'm escorted by two men, one in front and another behind me.

Mr. Big sits in his gilded chair. "I have a little bit of a rivalry with an associate. I want you to break into his shop and remove something from the premises."

I smile. "What is it?"

"The world's largest cubic zirconium."

My smile fades. "How many carats?"

"I don't know, but it weighs twenty-five pounds."

Gears turn in my head. This is what I need to get the adrenals working. "Do you have a floor layout? Alarm system?"

"I got nothing. Is that a deal-breaker?"

"No, I like a challenge." I need the challenge. I crave the challenge.

Mr. Big throws his head back and laughs. "Ya know, you have a relaxed attitude for a guy being held against his will."

"I'm on vacation, so call it part of the adventure. I don't want to sound racist, but you're a troll. I've never met a troll with a mean bone in their body. I know you won't lay a finger on Pam, but I'll do the job anyway because it sounds like fun."

"You know a lot of trolls?"

I think for a minute. "Twenty. My hometown has a subdivision near the water."

"Seattle."

"Ceres."

"Yeah, I've heard of it."

I change the subject. "When is sunset?"

51

"Why, you gonna turn into a bat?" Drucilla asks.

I feel playful and say, "Is that a deal-breaker?"

She gives me a sniff. "What's that smell? Cookie dough cologne?"

Mr. Big smiles. "Drucilla has taken a shine to you. She'll be your driver tonight." He stands up and then pats my butt hard.

I step forward to recover my balance, then follow Drucilla to the exit.

"Can we at least go to my hotel room to get a change of clothes?" I ask.

Drucilla escorts me into my room while a man built like a vending machine stands outside.

I take off my new jacket and hang it up.

Drucilla checks out my wardrobe. It's mainly three-piece suits, except for the outfit she pulls out. "What is this?"

"That's a classic black cocktail dress. Technically, it's a sheath dress because it's a fitted, straight-cut garment."

"With butt padding?"

"To accentuate my narrow waistline."

She holds the dress against my body. "Where do you wear it?"

"Lesbian bars."

"You pick up chicks in lesbian bars." Drucilla's raised eyebrow suggests she's either impressed, confused, incredulous or a combination of all three.

"Victoria is a babe magnet."

"I'd like to see you wear it."

I wag my finger. "No, no, no. Victoria requires wining and dining. You'll have to seduce her."

Drucilla puts the dress back and smiles. "So, what happens when your date brings you home and checks under the hood."

I return her smile. "Nine out of ten times, it's not a deal breaker."

"You're bat shit crazy."

"Victoria sleeps with women way above my pay grade."

"What about the redhead? She's a cutie. I smell her on you; you had sex."

"Breakup sex, sorta. We only went out once. It was probably more like, 'on vacation sex,' and we will never speak of it again."

"That happens a lot in Las Vegas." Drucilla takes a step back. "Watch my Sigma 4.8 power."

She wiggles her hips, and a wave passes through her waist, sending ripples up and down her body. Her skirt falls to the ground, and her top follows. Drucilla has ample breasts with the

most petite nipples I've ever seen.
They're the size of pink dimes.

"You're... callipygian. Nice, but it
doesn't feel right because I was just
with another woman."

"I know, it's a terrible moral
dilemma." She grabs my hand and
kisses my fingers. "If there is only some
way that I can ease this torture you are
going through. If only there was some
way I could help you to relax."

Drucilla puts my hand against
her chest. She's playing the role of Inga
from *Young Frankenstein*, a black-and-
white movie. It's very arousing.

Drucilla's tongue finds mine. She
recoils, spits, then laughs. "Wow, my
saliva glands are cramping." She wags
her nimble tongue, then wipes it off on
the bedsheet. "How can something that
smells so sweet taste so sour?"

She doesn't wait for me to answer. Instead, she flops on the bed and rolls her round bottom back and forth. "Vould you like to have a roll in ze hay?"

Drucilla is an enthusiastic lover and spanker. I hold her hands down so I can focus. It only increases her excitement.

*   *   *

I get dressed in my thieving clothes: jeans, a long-sleeved black t-shirt, running shoes, and a vest with many pockets. I run my fingers over them, check the inventory, put on my ball cap, and look at Drucilla.

She's brushing tangles out of her hair.

"Are you ready, Drucilla?"

"My friends call me Drew," she says, putting away her hairbrush. Drew's purse is a cloth produce bag from a local market. She pulls out a padded pouch with a Velcro flap; it looks worn. "This is for the gem. Those two have been stealing the glitzy rock from each other for a decade. It's a game to them."

We walk out, and the vending machine man gives me a smirk. He leads us to the staff entrance, where a black four-door sedan awaits. I get in the back seat and close the door. Drucilla sits in the front passenger seat.

"Autopilot, drive," she says.

The air is chill. It's the perfect evening for a little thievery. It's like shopping, but everything is free, and you rarely know what you'll get.

"So, you're a thief. How's that working out for you?"

I like banter before a job. It gets my juices flowing. "The hours are good. Excellent pay. What is it exactly that you do for a living?" I ask.

Drew leans over the seat, pushing up her breasts.

The autopilot asks Drew to put her seat belt on. She's pissed because it keeps asking every two minutes.

"Fine, Fine, Fine!" she yells, putting the seat belt on while facing me. Drew's dexterity is impressive. She repositions her breasts and says, "What were we talking about?"

"What knockers," I say, quoting Dr. Frankenstein.

She smiles demurely. "Thank you, Doctor."

"You like horror movies?" I ask.

"I love horror. Did you know that people who enjoy being scared are happier? I think it's the hormone rush."

"Horror isn't scary enough for me. I need real danger to get my juices flowing."

Drew cocks her head to one side. "Really, you want to see something terrifying."

I sit up straighter. "Oh yeah, show me what you've got."

She cocks her head at an unnatural angle and pulls back her lips, exposing her teeth. Her canines extend two inches and excrete a blue viscous substance. Without taking her eyes off mine, she pours her body over her backrest, onto the back seat, and into my lap in a single, fluid motion. Drew mimics the sound of a rattlesnake and rears back her head, exposed fangs dripping.

I lightly pinch her nipples, and she giggles. "That tickles. I should have never revealed my kryptonite."

59

Our very conspicuous four-door sedan pulls into an alley and parks behind a shop. I get out and set up a pin light behind a dumpster to cast a shadow across the door. I would pick the lock but I don't want Drucilla to follow.

I put on my goggles, lean down and put my hand in the shadow. I feel the cold and let it take me in. The void scatters my atoms and thoughts for a single heartbeat, and then, in the next beat, I'm on the other side of the door.

I survey the loading dock. It's the size of a two-car garage and filled with wooden crates. A quick scan reveals no motion sensors. Before I step, the door opens behind me, bumping my ass.

Drucilla walks in. "The door's unlocked."

I check for a magnetic switch in the doorjamb. Finding nothing, I close it. "An unlocked door is a bad sign," I whisper. "Might mean they have a dog or something."

"Six Sigma can take care of a dog." Drucilla crosses to the opposite door and opens it.

I follow, noting that the stairs to our right head up. Drucilla strolls around like she's shopping.

I put my hand on her shoulder. "Where's the CZ?"

"What?"

"Cubic zirconium."

"Upstairs, third floor, that's where all the weird stuff is kept."

"Then what are we doing here?" I whisper.

"I like the crystals. Is that ruby?"

"No, that's Cuprite crystal. A ruby that size would be in a museum."

"They have nice stones, but Mr. Big won't let me shop here." Drucilla touches, sniffs and licks every crystal. She puts the ones she likes in her shopping bag filled with socks. To prevent them from getting scratched, she puts them in a stockings.

I get impatient, take her by the hand and pull her to the steps. Reluctantly, she climbs to the third floor.

The two flights of stairs allow me time to carefully study Drucilla's physique. She moves like her bones are mostly cartilage, flowing and sensual.

At the top is an Ancient Egyptian exhibit. There is an open sarcophagus complete with a mummy. A foot-wide cubic zirconium is displayed behind velvet ropes. Low-level lasers bounce light off its surface. It is a glittery and flamboyant display that's perfect for Las Vegas.

Before entering the area, I look for cameras.

"Hey!" Drucilla yells. She's on the floor by the mummy. "Somebody just tripped me."

"Shhh. Use your indoor voice." I check behind us.

Only the emergency exit sign and laser lights illuminate the room.

"No one's there. Look, you tripped over a statue." I pick up a plaster of Paris statue of Isis and its now detached headdress and put them back on a shelf, making a mental note to add a tube of superglue to my kit.

Then I reach for her hand and help Drew to her feet. She must have hit the wall with some force because a mosaic tile tumbles to the floor with a clatter. I walk over and notice a box in the exposed cavity.

"What's that?" Drucilla asks.

"It's a Japanese puzzle box," I say as my fingers instantly go to work. I've always been good with manual dexterity skills. In a few minutes, the box is open.

"Holy shit, is that an emerald?" Drucilla yells.

I put my hand over her mouth. She licks it, then gags and spits. After wiping my hand, I inspect the gem. It's the same size as the star sapphire held by the Kukan dragon statue. It must belong to one of the five dragons. For a few seconds, I'm tempted to keep it, but I remember the trouble with the sapphire. I duck under the velvet ropes, stuff the cubic zirconium into my backpack and put the emerald in its place.

"Aren't you going to take it?"

"I got what we came for," I say, placing the puzzle box in a vest pocket.

Blue lights flash on the walls. I check a nearby window and spot a police car pulling up out front. The area is lit by standard red LEDs; the interference patterns set up shadows through the window.

I take Drucilla by the hand. "You ready to leave."

"Yeah, sigma six me."

I let the shadows embrace us while Drucilla's panic is shredded to nothingness. We emerge a block away, at a street corner. Drucilla wobbles, and I stand close for support. In a few minutes, she recovers and sends a text. Soon, our car shows up, and we get in.

Drucilla gets behind the wheel and punches the gas. The four-door sedan was made for trolls, so it has heavy suspension and a sluggish response.

"That was the biggest rush of my life," she says.

I take off the backpack and settle into the backseat. "That was fun, and it wasn't really stealing; it's a prank."

"What about the puzzle box in your pocket."

I smile. "That's payment. Tell Mr. Big to put it on the expense account. Although, if you do that, you should come clean about the gems in your bag."

She shrugs. "That ain't gonna happen."

We stop at a red light, and a man walks across the street. He stops, looks at Drucilla and reaches into his jacket pocket. She accelerates, spinning the wheels. The man moves aside and shoots at the driver's window. The plexiglass buckles but doesn't break. He takes another shot, targeting the back window this time. The result is the same.

As we drive away, the man clotheslines someone on a motorcycle. While the helmeted rider is stretched out on the pavement, he gets on the bike.

"Who's that?"

Drew runs the next light and makes a hard left. "My crazy ex-boyfriend, Dmitri."

"Crazy, how?" I ask as the motorcycle turns off the main road and closes in.

"I think he's a triple agent for the Russians and Mossad. Dmitri has multiple personalities, and each seems to work for a different agency."

Another round pings against the back window. I crawl into the passenger seat.

"We'll ditch the car and go underground," she says.

"What about Caesars Palace?"

"We won't get within three blocks before Dmitri's men mow us down with machine guns." She looks in the back seat. "You'll want to grab that gem."

"I have to haul a 25-pound rock?" I ask while reaching over the back seat.

"It's a matter of honor."

"Roger that," I say. Trolls would rather lose money than respect.

Another round hits the back window.

Drucilla turns down an alley barely wide enough for the sedan. Ahead is a chain-link fence. She stops a few feet short. We crawl out the windows and hop on the hood as another round whizzes past. Drucilla slides off and tries to pull up a drainage grate. It's stuck. She looks at me.

Usually, I'm not the go-to guy for muscle sports, but my recent augments changed that. I yank it, and the grate comes up. Drucilla hops down the hole while Dmitri gets off his bike. I follow; the tunnel is only three feet high. I replace the cover. Maybe Dmitri won't notice our exit route. It's unlikely, but a small chance is better than none.

We're inside a brick drainage culvert circa 1800s. Crouching, we walk slightly downhill, passing other tributaries, until there's enough headroom for us to stand upright. Pipes leading to the surface provide spotlights of illumination.

I retrieve my goggles from my vest pocket and put them on. Cockroaches scurry across the arched ceiling. Their antennae wiggle as we pass beneath them.

Behind us, a foot kicks a pebble. The sound echoes off the bricks. Drucilla picks up the pace. In minutes, the passage widens again. As we enter an underground train station converted into a mall, a stench of vomit and stale beer is in the air. Knowing where to go, I remove my goggles and take Drucilla's hand. The temperature is in the mid-sixties, and everyone wears jackets. A sign says 'no hats,' which means cameras are watching.

Dmitri is looking for a man in black with a backpack and his ex-girlfriend. I duck into a clothing store, and a middle-aged man in a goatee beard greets us. I hand him a half-ounce gold coin. "We need everything but shoes."

Within twenty minutes, we're ready for the Las Vegas underground scene. I'm in slacks with a sharp crease, a white long-sleeved shirt, and a spider silk vest. To hide the bulges, I wear a sports jacket on top. Drucilla wears an exceptionally hip-hugging knee-length dress with an interactive fake fur coat that accents her breasts and shows off her waist. It's not my first choice for a getaway outfit, but she looks great. I get a free cloth shopping bag with the store logo and put the cubic zirconium inside. Still, lugging a 25-pound rock is conspicuous.

I look at the mall legend and find a FedEx twelve stores down. I pay a few hundred credits to have the cubic zirconium delivered by courier. Since Caesars is only a few miles away, it's guaranteed to arrive within the hour.

I take Drew's hand and blend in with the crowd.

A few shops down, they're selling people. A dozen are lined up against the glass storefront. The sign claims they're androids, but they're not. Androids have perfect skin and teeth. These men and women look drugged and are dressed in skimpy outfits. Drucilla senses my discomfort and pulls me away from the storefront. She quickly whisks me past the sex district into a section specializing in augments.

One shop claims it can turn you into a special operations super soldier. I check the list: muscle and bone augment, cyber eyes and ears, plus a Mark 6 implant with artificial intelligence that's an expert in dozens of weapons. I shrug. I got my augments at the Navy hospital for half the price— although the cyber eyes they're advertising are a generation ahead of mine.

We find a chocolate store and restaurant and get a table close to the kitchen with a clear view of the entrance. Now I can relax. When hiding from an enemy, it is vital to blend in. It also helps to know who your enemy is.

"Tell me about Dmitri?"

"He left me in a lurch. I caught him in our favorite restaurant nine months later with another woman."

A waiter who resembles Ed Sullivan delivers coffee and a pile of triple-thick chocolate brownies. "May I bring you anything else?"

With the war in South America, it isn't easy to find chocolate, except in Vegas.

"I'll take two kilos of chocolate bars and a kilo of your cocoa mix. I look at the neat stack of ten brownies. Their cocoa content is so high they look black. "I might need a to-go bag."

I hand Ed Sullivan a half-ounce silver coin as a tip. He breaks character for a second and smiles.

Drucilla beams at me, and I forget why we're here for a moment, imagining I'm out on the town with an attractive woman in a pretty dress, deliberately showing me plenty of cleavage. Life doesn't get better than this. Then, a man walks in with a similar build to the bad guy, and I'm jarred back to reality.

"So, Dmitri, does he have a temper?"

"Yes, I used his credit card and didn't tell him, and he smashed the kitchen table to bits with one blow."

"Has he ever hurt you?"

"No, but he wanted to, really bad."

"So, you saw him at your favorite restaurant. What happened."

"I had a conceal carry permit, so I shot him."

I raise an eyebrow. Not one to judge, I say something neutral. "You shot him." All those years with the school counselor come in handy.

Drucilla shrugs her shoulders. "Just in the foot, and it was a .22, a small hole."

I nod. "A friendly flesh wound."

She giggles. "Okay, I overreacted, but he's not interested in listening to my apology. You can handle Dmitri. Your mutant power is six standard deviations from normal."

"I have some amazing abilities under a very narrow bandwidth of conditions. I work best with a lot of open ground. Closed-in underground is not a favorable terrain."

"So, you can't do your thing in this lighting?"

I nod. "Exactly."

"Maybe we should get to the surface."

"Yeah, let's do that."

Drew heads to the bathroom when the chocolate bars and cocoa arrive. I pay the bill with my Rick Savage debit card and load the four remaining brownies in the to-go bag. Then I get a bad feeling. I leave the food by the till and head to the bathroom. I crack the door a little and listen. There's a man's voice. Before I can react, someone puts a pistol near my left kidney. I raise my hands and am shoved through the door. Inside, Dmitri has Drew pinned against a wall with a pistol at her heart. His finger is not on the trigger. They both look at me for a second. Drew's eyes plead for help.

"He won't save you. Answer the question. I told you I dated other women. I told you I travel nine months a year and don't want a commitment. You said you were fine with that, so why did you shoot me?"

Drew's eyes are as big as saucers.

Dmitri is yelling and acting angry, but his hands are steady. He leans his weight into the pistol, pressing Drew into the wall.

"She was prettier than me," Drew screams. "I turn twenty-one and am already too old. How old was that blonde bitch? Fourteen?"

Dmitri lowers the gun. "Seventeen."

"You sent me a breakup text. Are you too busy or too important to break up in person?"

He puts away his pistol. "I see. This is entirely my fault."

He and his buddy walk away, leaving Drucilla and me alone in the bathroom. Drucilla can barely look at me. I expect it's too much, airing all her dirty laundry on a first date.

"Would you like a drink? Something stronger than cocoa?" I ask.

Drew nods, and I lead her out of the bathroom. We find our way back to the underground mall. I check the legend and find a bar with live music. After a few minutes and a silver dollar tip, we sit in a booth. Drew still can't make eye contact with me. Instead, she stares at her drink.

"I've pulled some crazy stunts, too. Put a croc in the high school swimming pool, stole a liquid nitrogen truck, and tormented people with my intellect just because they told me what to do."

Drew looks up. "How dare they?"

I nod. "Yeah, have you noticed how people with the most screwed up lives are the same ones who know exactly how to run yours?"

Another round of drinks arrives.

"So, you don't hate me?"

"No. You said it yourself, you overreacted, you're sorry, and you won't do it again."

"I can't. They took away my conceal carry permit."

I shrug my shoulders. "What? For a teeny tiny twenty-two hole. You put a band-aid on that and walk it off."

Drew giggles, and the music starts. It's a slow song.

"Do you want to dance?" Drew asks.

We head onto the dance floor with other couples. A man with a guitar and a hologram of a woman with a harp sing a Lord Huron song, The Night We Met.

Drew leans into me, and I hold her. We stand in the same spot and sway to the music. When the song ends, we return to our booth and spend the rest of the night chatting. At 5 AM, management kicks us out.

"Are you going back to Caesars Palace?" Drew asks.

"No, I just stole the world's largest cubic zirconium, and I'm sure face-recognition software has alerted the police."

She pokes a bulge in my vest pocket. "And the puzzle box."

"Thank you for a lovely evening."

She smiles. "This is, by far, the strangest first date ever."

"Third strangest first date for me."

She laughs, and then we kiss. I watch her walk away until she's lost in the crowd.

"Natasha, start the pre-flight check."

Before I leave Vegas, I phone Pam's hotel. "It's me."

"Hermes, I just..." I can tell from the tone of her voice she's been worrying.

"I'm fine."

"About this morning..."

"What happens in Vegas stays in Vegas," I assure her. "I'm glad we have *closure.*"

There is a pause, and then Pam says, "Yes, closure."

I smile. "It's best I leave town. For the record, I know we're not right for each other, but that doesn't mean I love you any less."

"I know."

"I'll see you back home." I hang up. A cab pulls up beside me. "Thanks, Natasha."

Chapter Five

Ten minutes later, I'm in the private screening area. Two more minutes, and I'm heading to the hangar. The F16 engine is running, and the stairs on wheels are parked. I climb up, get inside, and the cowling moves into place.

After I put on the helmet, the jet approaches the taxiway. After a short wait, we are cleared to depart.

Once we're in the air, Natasha says, *"I like Vegas. There are plenty of opportunities for sexual encounters."*

"That was kind of weird."

"Because of your feelings for Pam?"

"Yeah."

"I sent Drew a text thanking her for her hospitality."

Soon, we're on approach. The console flashes red—RADAR LOCK. An alarm buzzes in the cockpit. Instantly, I'm pushed back into my seat from the acceleration as the jet dives into a thicker atmosphere to bleed energy from the rocket heading our way. The G-force seat inflates the cuffs around my legs to prevent my blood from pooling. I'm pinned back for what seems like hours, and then there's a roll and a hard right. Chaff is expelled to confuse the missile's radar, and flare light flashes to draw its infrared. The rocket zooms past the window.

I blackout for a few seconds during the next maneuver. When I come, the front sights have weapons lock and a missile on the right-wing zooms away. Soon, there is a flash, and the RADAR LOCK indicator turns off. The F16's radar illuminates a missile battery hiding under a tree canopy. There are four targets. One is blown up, probably the radar array. While I read the displays, another missile launches, taking out the vehicle carrying missiles. Explosions erupt. The F16 circles the site. The infrared camera shows people emerging from nearby cover in a few minutes. The megawatt laser turns each one into a puff of steam.

When the F16 autopilot ensures the threat is neutralized, it disengages combat mode and lines up for the final approach into Ceres. The plane lands without incident before taxiing to the hangar. After I alight, the jet turns around and takes off.

My electric truck is waiting for me in the parking lot. I back out and head down the road. My father once told me to concentrate exclusively on those things I can influence when events seem out of control. It was good advice and helps me keep a clear head. Driving along these country roads toward home, with the heat on and the windows open, reminds me of this. It's also a great form of meditation. Instead of a fear hangover, I feel happy to have survived another attack.

I know there will be more to come. I spent a year stuck inside Ceres, building resentment until I went stir-crazy. Those two days in Vegas made me feel like myself again, even if I needed to cut my vacation short. The missile attack on my way home means Baron's men are doing their job. If it wasn't for Natasha's almost paranoid security measures, we would be dead, but she's a part of me, and anyone who comes for me must go through her. Baron's men will have no vulnerabilities to report this time.

Natasha appears next to me. *"Are you okay?"*

"Yeah. Colonel James is right. Jason Baron hates me."

Part Two

Fall of Ceres

Chapter Six

I catch myself humming as I clear the breakfast things. The lingering happiness is a delightful side effect of my Vegas vacation. Natasha appears while I'm loading the dishwasher. She sits on the counter, looking smart and sexy in her secretary's outfit. The knee-length brown pencil skirt skims her thighs, and the buttons of her long-sleeved blouse strain to accommodate her chest. A neat bun and glasses complete the look. I'm sure Freud would have a field day. Functionally, neural implants don't need to be gorgeous, but it definitely makes interacting with them more fun.

"Darling, do you recall a conversation about using rules to our best advantage?"

"You mean exploiting the law to make money?"

Natasha gives me an adorable smile and a tablet computer appears in her hand. *"I studied the Native Rights Act that gives Trolls habitation and income rights from the Sacramento Bayou."*

I nod. Trolls are amphibious. They love water, and the wetlands are their natural home.

"Recently, the owners of various rice patents sued a community of trolls living in the Florida Everglades. They were selling genetically engineered rice at a farmer's market. The court ruled partially in favor of the trolls—they can sell patented rice without paying license fees but are not allowed to use heavy

equipment. *Engines are limited to five horsepower.*"

"How does this benefit us? There are dozens of rice strains in the public domain and little to no money to be made."

"True, but something else grows in semi-brackish water."

My eyebrows rise as I realize what Natasha's getting at. "The bladderwrack seaweed used for making diesel oil?"

Natasha smiles. *"The new varieties grow in salt and fresh water."*

"How do we get a sample?"

"From my contacts at the University of Frisco."

"Your contacts?"

Natasha slides her butt off the counter, walks over, and plays with my hair. *"North of the Bayou are two hundred square miles of sawgrass. We* funded a study into the uses of sawgrass in building construction."

"I'm confused. Why did we fund a sawgrass study?"

She sighs and makes that face she always wears when she explains something simple to me. *"To make friends at the University of Frisco, Agriculture Department, aka my contacts."*

"Okay, I'm following you, but I don't imagine we'll make much money turning seaweed into diesel?

She smiles. *"We purchased two hundred square miles of sawgrass harvesting rights on federal land."*

"You spent my money without asking first?"

"I know how upset you get when I spend money. I made all the arrangements."

"How much?"

"One point eight million credits."

I cough up some coffee. Natasha tuts as she cleans the spill before it can stain my shirt. Of course, she can't sponge it off, so I get up and take care of it.

I sit back and stare at her. "When will we see a profit?"

"Three years to pay back. We should double our money before the lease expires."

"Have you found a buyer for the twin-engine Cessna Eagle?"

Natasha pouts. *"Yes."*

"I know it's your second love, but we are grounded for a long time."

She crosses her arms. *"Flying is my first love."*

"First time ever I saw your nosecone," I sing to the tune of the Roberta Flack song.

Natasha smiles and then forces a frown.

"As soon as we aren't being hunted, we'll get a better plane. You're the one who's all about security. That's why I retired from show biz."

"Are you mad at me?"

"No, I miss holding a camera and taunting big guys into running after me. And you miss flying. We've both lost something important."

"Let's go to the berry festival," Natasha says. *"That will put us in a better mood."*

While holding my coffee, I use my foot to push the button that opens my front door. It's a refurbished bank vault door. An electric motor hums and the door opens. More importantly, the chromium looks really cool.

Outside, everything is green. I don't like cutting grass, so I planted

Dutch white clover. It grows best under the shade of trees. It's June, and the oranges are ripening. The apples will be ready in October. Natasha opens the first bay in the 3-car garage, and I get in my electric truck. I pull out and turn right onto Main Street. The town center is only a mile away, and I poke along at under 15 miles an hour, slowing down when a neighbor's peacock flies across the road.

A four-meter median with genetically engineered oak trees was constructed to hide traffic from drones. Along the edges, there are black cherry trees. By the end of the year, they'll reach thirty feet. I continue straight through the intersection of Main and Baker Street. One kilometer later, I pull into the high school parking lot. It's full. A man in a yellow vest shows me where to park on the soccer field. It's a little after ten, and the party is already in full swing.

They built a twelve-foot-high chain link fence around the perimeter when Ceres was founded. School kids have added extra thorny raspberry and blackberry bushes over the years. The plants intertwine in the chain link and make an impressive barrier. People pick berries for wine, beer, ale, pies, and jams.

I weave through the crowd and follow my nose to a burger stand. Soon, I'm served and find a spot under an oak tree and munch on my burger and fries. I spot Kim and wave.

She comes over and sits next to me. "Vanya got a steady fuck now."

"You mean boyfriend."

"Did you get laid in Vegas?" she asks.

I continue chewing. I'm used to Kim's coarseness, and it's no longer amusing, but the woman has a big heart despite her brash way of talking. She's a telepath. Thankfully, since I got my implant, Kim hasn't been able to read my mind. Maggie's teaching Kim techniques to read the unreadable: ask a question and study the reaction, use that information to ask a follow-up question, and slowly wear people down until they spill their secrets.

"Natasha tells me you rented a stretch limo, picked up hookers on the street corner and fucked them in the back seat. Do you know what would be better? Bone them on the hood and run the car through a wash when you are through." Kim studies my face.

I open my mouth to speak, then insert a French fry.

"Since you can't get STDs, you can probably skip the hose. It's inefficient." Kim punches my shoulder. "Tell me, did you fuck Pam? Because she came home with a smile on her face." Kim studies me carefully, trying to read my expression.

I give her my slack-jawed look.

"Pam's been kissing that tall hunk of a man, Jessie."

I hate Jessie Stevens. I don't know why women are all over him. If you remove his rugged good looks, charming personality and hundred-and-eighty IQ, he's a hollow shell of a man.

"Yeah, he's boning her."

"None of my business," I say and finish the burger.

Kim stands up and places her hands on her hips. "You got no chance of getting laid in this town with Vanya and Pam out of the picture. I'll let you play with my tits while I give you a hand job."

"As tempting as that may sound, I saw you crush the metal top of a beer stein, so I'm gonna pass."

The announcer says the pie-eating contest is starting.

"Gotta go," Kim says. "Vike's competing."

I wipe my fingers on the grass. "Always good catching up with you, Kim."

Kim points at me and winks. "Right back at ya."

I watch her ass while she walks away.

Colonel James sits in the soccer bleachers, talking to John. James runs the town via mini-meetings. He puts someone in charge of a project, allows them to pick their own team, and the mission is compartmentalized. Only

Colonel James and maybe his second in command, Major Hayes, know everything. I can tell a lot is going on by the number of people queuing to see him.

After John leaves, I sit next to the Colonel. "I have a job. Are you interested?"

"Yes," Colonel James replies.

"Remember last year when I told you I'd acquired a key to a safety deposit box during the Partisan Rangers raid? Natasha has done some research, and it belongs to Samuel Pérez, the seventy-two-year-old retired CEO of Centaur Motors, who currently resides in Florida while recovering from a mild stroke. His boyfriend was carrying the key while on a fishing trip. If I had to guess, I'd say he was planning to steal Samuel's money and vanish. If so, he only achieved half his plan because he did disappear. The Partisan Rangers killed and ate him."

The Colonel traces his finger down a scar on his cheek. "How do you know it still works?"

"I don't know for sure, but Natasha hacked into the locksmith that services the safety deposit boxes. According to the files, an extra key was made, but there was no charge for a new core for the safety deposit box."

"How do you know his box number?"

"Because Natasha also hacked into the Northwest Bank's computer."

"Okay, what do you need from me?"

"A ride to and from Northwest Bank."

"And what's so special about this particular safety deposit box?"

"My gut says it's a big score."

"Can't argue with your gut. Your father has good money-making instincts. That's why he's my first sergeant."

"You mean your go-to guy."

"You two are so different yet so alike."

"We're both thieves, but I prefer non-violent methods."

"True. But you're both very good at violence."

I stare at my feet. "Yeah."

Colonel James pats my shoulder. "If you feel bad, it means you have a conscience." He changes the subject. "We have a lead on Jason Baron's lawyer. His name is Ronald Fulton, and he likes hookers."

I smile. "Where does he hang out?"

"Blood Relations."

My smile widens. "The vampire club."

"Know any hooker vampires?" Colonel James asks.

"Crushed Velvet, The Pop and Fresh Twins, Arkham Horror and Fox Force Five are available for parties."

He closes his eyes. "Your Frisco Nights contacts, of course."

"Have you seen my show?"

"Only your knife fight video. You're good. Be careful, or you'll attract the attention of people who want to kill you to build their reputations."

My grin dies, and I change the subject. "Tomorrow's a full moon."

"We intercepted Fulton's text messages. He made reservations for a booth at Blood Relations for tonight.

"Okay, I'll make some calls. Thanks."

When I leave, another takes my place. Colonel James has a busy morning ahead.

Striding back to the truck, my mental gears grind. "Natasha, take down the knife fight video."

"*Roger that*," she replies.

* * *

Stevens sits on my kitchen barstool. He gazes into a mirror while using a phone app to check his skin color.

"It's a good outdoor-in-the-sun look," I say. "Now pop into the accessory menu and pick *scar, eye, vertical.*"

A dark scar appears above his eyebrow and stops halfway down his cheek. I get out the makeup kit and use a highlighter on his eyebrows. "Now watch. It will take a few minutes."

The middle of Stevens' eyebrow gradually lightens to grey along the scar's path.

"A vertical line across the eye disrupts facial recognition software. You look like a Murdock, but who is Murdock?"

"You're into this acting thing," he grumbles.

"Speaking of acting, here are a few pointers for tonight. First, try not to act like a Navy pilot. Don't say: 'Bravo Zulu,' 'Roger that,' or 'what-the-fuck, over,' and have your backstory ready."

"Backstory?"

"You can't go into a vampire club without a backstory. Who is Murdock? How did he get the scar? Blood Relations keeps the music down so people can talk. You need to be entertaining with your words. None of this monosyllabic nonsense."

104

"Sounds like you spend a lot of time in vampire clubs?"

I put my hand on my chest. "Me? No, never. When it comes to sex, I'm a meat-and-potatoes kind of guy. However, Mr. Wong has some exotic tastes." Time to get in character. "Natasha, change my face to Michael Wong's."

The liquid crystals attached to my facial bones expand and morph my features. The process takes a few minutes, and it itches.

"Darling, you have a call."

The Pop and Fresh Twins appear on the screen, voluptuously pale women, currently wearing bathrobes and oozing sex. "Hi, Michael; who's that handsome man with you?"

"Murdock," Stevens says.

The twin in the pink bathrobe says, "I'm Pop. They call me that because I go off at the slightest touch."

The red bathrobe says, "I'm Fresh, and I'm very tactile." Her voice sounds like a purr.

Stevens' eyes glaze.

I keep my chuckle inside my head and get down to business. "A man named Fulton will be at Blood Relations tonight. I want you to show him a good time and lift his work ID so Murdock can make a copy."

"That's extra," the twins say in unison.

Natasha links to their website and transfers three thousand credits from one of our shell companies.

"See you at eight." Pop ends the call.

Next, I text Arkham Horror. "I'm bringing a newbie."

"I owe you," she replies.

Arkham Horror is an extraordinary empath who can broadcast terror to anyone within sixty feet. Vampires and their clients love it. I suppose the mix of sex and fear heightens the entire experience.

"Natasha, rent a booth. Make the reservation under Michael Wong."

While Stevens puts in his contact lenses, I head upstairs and change into three layers of armor: spider silk, a vest with bullet-resistant panels, and a long sleeve shirt. A drone will be in the air during the operation, so I pop on my new wireless spectacles, configured for text and voice. The bandwidth is kept low so it won't overheat my ears, meaning Natasha will have direct access to the Colonel when the high-speed fiber optic port is connected. A pair of formal trousers and a dinner jacket with microsensors woven into the fabric complete my outfit. The jacket has sensors that detect light, microwaves and infrared. A fiber optic cable in the collar plugs into my glasses, giving Natasha eyes behind us.

I smile into the mirror, and Natasha appears dressed in black leather. Her sandy blonde hair is in a bun held in place with chopsticks. *"I've never been to a vampire club."*

"You'll love it, lots of talk and flirting."

"And petting?" Natasha asks.

I smile. "A little bit. If you want to return when we aren't on the job, they have back rooms for rent. Personally, I prefer people-watching. Just about anyone can show up."

I return downstairs. Stevens is checking himself in the front door mirror. His vest is covered in tiny scales, each the size of a dime.

"It doesn't have pockets," I say.

"The scales stop 30-caliber rounds."

I check the gear in my pockets one last time and press the button to open the front door.

Stevens and I get in the car and head to the south gate, joined by three other vehicles. Forty minutes later, the Frisco gate guard checks our ID and lets the convoy pass through.

We drive downtown and split up. Our driver takes us to a parking garage, where we pull in next to a full-size sedan. Stevens and I get out and switch cars.

I text Arkham. "Murdock is a tall, dark man with a scar on the right eye."

"What exactly is a vampire?" Stevens asks.

109

"Mutants who feed on emotions, sexual desire mostly. The Pop and Fresh twins emit powerful pheromones, making them irresistible. Most Emo vampires are either telepathic, empathic or something else. They're an interesting subspecies."

Stevens says, "We have implants to protect us from telepaths."

I smile. "Telepaths, but not empaths."

The car stops outside Blood Relations, and I lead through the entrance. My cyber eyes quickly adjust to the low light. Security is strict. Our only weapons are plastic knuckles that pass through the scanner undetected. We're not expecting trouble, but if something happens, our spider silk undergarments can stop knives, and our vests will stop a few rounds of ammo before disintegrating.

An elf hostess takes us to our reserved booth while Emo vampires in cocktail dresses flirt with customers.

I lean over to Stevens. "Vampires pay a fee to work the club for the night. You keep paying for their drinks, and they'll flirt at your table. If they ask you for money for the bathroom, it's fifty credits or a silver dollar. Usually, fifty credits an hour will keep a vampire at your table."

Within minutes, Pop and Fresh show up, wearing bikinis a size too small under their monogrammed bathrobes.

Pop slides over to me. "Michael, we haven't seen you in a while. Fresh thought you were dead, but I've watched you roll six boxcars in a row, so I knew you'd be back."

I whisper into her ear. "I came for you."

Pop has a condition called Autonomous Sensory Meridian Response. Crinkling paper or whispers give her a tingling feeling that slowly moves down her neck and spine.

"Tell me more," she purrs.

"I can't look at another woman because no one compares to you. It pains me to tell you that Fulton is talking to the receptionist because I know you must leave me."

She squeezes my thigh and gets up. "Fresh, time to go to work."

Fresh ignores her twin for a moment. She leans toward Stevens. "Since I'm touching you, it's only fair that you feel me." She moves Stevens' hand below the table.

"Fresh, save him for later; we're on the clock."

Fresh kisses Stevens' lips. "Later."

The twins glide over to Fulton; each takes an arm. They guide him to a booth and order drinks. Now, we wait for the twins to get Fulton's ID. Once that's done, Stevens and I can mingle.

Arkham Horror rolls her hips as she approaches our table. She's six-foot-tall, but in her six-inch heels and nine-inch horns, she towers over us. She's scantily dressed in orange hot pants and a cerise tube top. Her generous breasts are mere inches from his face when she leans over to Stevens.

"Murdock! I saw you with that hussy." Her voice drops an octave, and her skin turns crimson. "How dare you leave me!"

Then, she radiates horror. It's like a jolt of electricity to my gut. When you know what's happening, it's exhilarating, but it's Stevens' first time, and he's paralyzed. Arkham Horror and every Emo vampire within a sixty-foot radius feed on his terror.

She whispers in his ear before leaving our table.

"What's a three-hole?" Stevens asks.

"I always thought that was an urban legend, but with augments, who knows. What did she say?"

"My fear is sweet and juicy; you can poke my three-hole anytime."

"It's Arkham Horror, so it could be anywhere."

Stevens shudders. More drinks arrive, and we watch the eye candy while we sip.

Fresh sits next to Stevens and passes him the ID under the table. Stevens pulls a cloner from his pocket and puts Fulton's ID card inside.

Fresh strokes his hair. "You poor thing. You're a powder keg ready to go off."

I leave them to it and head to the bar to order another vodka. My gut tells me something's wrong. I realize this feeling has nothing to do with the club; it's outside. In this part of town, drug dealers in trench coats frequent each intersection, but while driving through town, I saw no one like that or homeless people.

Two years ago, Jason Baron released a virus designed to kill mutants. The Mayor quarantined Frisco, trapping the population to make the cull more effective. The mutants rebelled and burned a good section of the city. Many lost their homes and had to live on the streets. Vagrants were ubiquitous in downtown Frisco, but now they've all vanished. Why?

I finish my shot and walk back to our booth. Fresh and Stevens are getting friendly.

"Is it done?" I ask.

Fresh smiles. "Done and done with no one the wiser."

"Why don't you give yourself a twenty percent tip and let me have some bro time with Murdock."

She kisses Stevens and leaves.

Stevens gets up. "Come on; let's go."

I nod towards the bulge at his crotch and smirk. "We've been here...." I check my virtual watch. "Forty minutes. Let's sit and enjoy the scenery while you recover."

"That's negatory. You are a high-value target, and I have a high-value item." Stevens puts his hand on my shoulder and guides me to the exit. The man has no sense of decency.

"No, No, it's not fair," I whine.

Curbside, I breathe in Frisco Bay air and listen to the pounding bass from nearby bars. Plenty of people are on the street, checking out the bar scene. So, why are alarm bells going off in my head? I mumble.

"What?" Stevens says.

"Something's wrong."

"Where are the bouncers?" Stevens asks, nodding in agreement.

"Let's move; we need to be gone."

We march away from the lighted entrance and hasten along the street, blending with the crowds. I plug my suit into my glasses, allowing Natasha total bandwidth. The signal strength makes my ears burn.

"*Darling, two bikers have pulled up to the club.*"

"Don't look back. A hit team is looking for us," I tell Stevens.

I reach into my pocket, pull out a silver half-dollar and stop beside a guy with a ball cap. I pay the man for his hat and give it to Stevens.

"Natasha, change my face."

"*Hermes, our ride is stuck behind an accident.*"

Stevens grabs my shoulder and pulls me into a bar. Knowing something is up, I head to the kitchen. We leave by the back door. I find a shadow, grip Stevens' shoulder, and wrap the darkness around us. When I practiced my standard moves on him, he took anti-nausea drugs and didn't throw up, but declined a second trip, making me promise never to make him shadow walk unless it is an emergency. I think this qualifies.

Two men appear in the alley. A third man on a motorbike drives toward us from the opposite direction. They meet in the middle. The two men walk past us, and the man on the bike lights a cigarette.

Stevens puts on his plastic knuckles, steps out of the shadow, and punches the biker on his nose. The man's head rocks back as he falls off the bike. Stevens rummages through his pockets and finds a pistol with a silencer. He takes the front seat. I clamber on behind him, and then we ride away.

"Hermes, someone is jamming the airwaves. I've lost contact with the drone and Colonel Baker."

We're in what used to be Inner City Gang Territory before the virus riots. Today, it's controlled by a dozen much smaller gangs. Stevens drives along side streets and alleys until trashcans roll out in front of us. Then, Stevens turns around, only to discover that half a dozen mutants have blocked our exit.

We get off the bike, and I approach the leader, whose scales are the size of quarters. "We ask permission to pass through."

"Leave the bike." He points down the alley. "The K Street Gang's turf starts in nine blocks, and they keep strange pets. Be careful."

"Roger that," Stevens says as we walk away. When we cover the first block without incident, I feel more confident and enjoy the ambiance.

"What are you humming?" Stevens asks.

"Shelter from the Storm."

"Why are you so happy?"

"It's a night out on the town, and we're guests for the next eight blocks."

"There's more city to cover after those eight blocks."

"The moon is casting shadows, and the city is lit by LEDs. So, they'll never find us. Besides, I'm juiced up from the vamp club and haven't had a night out since Vegas."

"Pam mentioned you bumped into each other in Vegas."

"Yeah, we cleared the air. I love her, but we're not right for each other."

"You do know we're dating," he says seriously.

I think he's concerned about my feelings. "Kim mentioned that you were 'boning Pam.'"

Stevens chuckles.

We approach an intersection. A lookout motions for us to stop. Two men on bikes drive by at twenty miles per hour. We hide in shadows, and they pass without spotting us. After we cross the intersection, we keep to the alleys.

"What are you doing?" Stevens asks.

"My patented zombie dance, the jerkiness keeps me on the edge of balance."

"Yeah, I can see that, but I don't understand why."

"It's good training. It takes a highly dexterous actor to do the zombie."

"You never answer a question. You always answer around the question."

"Tomorrow's a full moon. That means today is a good day; not as good as tomorrow, but good enough."

A shadow bisects the alley. I walk down the center, one-half of my body hidden in shadow. It looks like I'm walking on one leg.

"I see how you got your nickname, Spooky."

122

Soon, we leave the protected territory and reach a badly burned section of the city. Only the red traffic lights glow, and lumps of metal litter the blistered asphalt.

"Where are we headed?" Stevens asks.

"Troll Town. It's east a mile or two. The Hole in the Wall has the best clam chowder. See, I can answer a question."

"With embellishment."

This part of Frisco used to be filled with high-priced townhomes. Several blocks have been cleared of rubble, and tents have replaced the houses. Sections like these were cleared and looted during the virus riots. Outcast mutants have made their homes here. They don't fit into any single category. They aren't elves, dwarves, trolls or vampires, and they don't like strangers. What was once a soccer field is now a market with LED fairy lights strung up around and between booths. Trash litters the streets. We stay clear of the market and head downhill.

A mutant with five eyes around a flat nose blocks our path. "What are you humans doing here?" he asks from the hole in his throat, which serves as a mouth. He grips a club in his right paw and points it toward us menacingly.

Stevens throws an empty beer bottle at the mutant with a quick toss. It smashes against his nose, and he topples to the ground. I keep my eyes on his weapon as we walk around him, but he's out cold.

"Nice move," I say.

"You point your elbow at what you want to hit and then flick." Stevens demonstrates with another bottle.

"Darling, I'm picking up an increase in encrypted chatter. Also, your ride home has four flat tires. The traffic lights have been hacked, and it's jamming up traffic. It will take at least a half hour for backup to arrive."

"We need to find cover," I say.

Natasha displays a translucent map of the area. There's a supermarket nearby. We head toward it.

I strap low-light goggles around my forehead. The area is still lit, but my gut tells me that's about to change. I start jogging, and Stevens follows.

"What's going on."

"Natasha says encrypted messages have spiked in the last few minutes. Our ride has been vandalized, and help won't arrive for at least half an hour." Luckily, I always have a plan B.

This section is full of burnt high-rise buildings. They're conventional steel and concrete structures eight stories tall. Incinerated cars litter the streets, and safety glass beads have been swept into piles. The area still reeks of burnt plastic. We use the shadows to make our way to the supermarket. The parking lot protected the building from fire but not from looters. A three-wheeled car is jammed in the entrance. Stevens picks his way around the glass while I use shadows.

Two large holes in the ceiling let in moonlight. The windows are shattered, and the place stinks of stale bread and urine.

For me to shift through shadows, I need both light and darkness. Shadows that move, like the ones made by headlights, are no good. Like the Moon, The light source must be fixed or very slow-moving. That's why being inside is a good thing. But only if it's a big space with room to maneuver.

Once inside, the bad guys will need low-light goggles or a flashlight that announces their presence. Inside, I can hunt them. Like my father says, always have a Plan B and pick the battleground. I'm stacking the deck as much as possible in my favor.

There isn't much time to get a lay of the land before four assassins riding motorcycles approach. They carry tech nine pistols with 30-round clips and keep their helmets on when they dismount. Stevens checks the clip on his tech nine 30 rounds, but no spare clips. He shoots a round through one assassin's calf. Almost instantly, a barrage of bullets comes our way. We use the checkout counter as cover to slip deeper into the store. Boots crunch on the glass as they enter. We move toward one of the holes where a shaft of moonlight casts rich shadows. The men are probably trying to be quiet, but every step is accompanied by noise. It's like trying to tiptoe through dried leaves. Everyone is using low-light technology. No flashlights to spoil the shadows.

A long shadow from an empty shelf runs half the length of the store. As a man in a motorcycle helmet passes the other end of an aisle, I shift and reappear behind him. I put my hand on his shoulder. His terror floods my consciousness. A few seconds later, we stand on the roof, looking down through a hole.

The assassin removes his helmet to vomit. While he's still reeling with vertigo, I grab his helmet and pistol and gently push him. He lands with a hard thud. Usually, spider silk armor stiffens to cushion the blow, but he landed on his head. I shift back to Stevens and hand him the second tech nine. With a pistol in each hand, Stevens smiles.

I inspect the helmet and find a USB port. I pull a cable from my vest pocket and plug one end behind my ear and the other into the helmet. Within seconds, Natasha hacks the software.

"Darling, I have the GPS coordinates of the bad guys, two inside and two more outside. The one Jessie shot has taken pain meds."

Two assassins are trying to flank us. One comes from the north, and the other from the south. I point, and Stevens takes the lead. He has zero stealth. Stevens steps on every wrapper and stale cracker in our path.

I flit from shadow to shadow. I check my pockets for my trusty knife before remembering the no-weapons-in-vampire-clubs rule and cursing myself for not searching the guy before I pushed him over the edge. I have problems with impulse control.

There is a method to Stevens' madness. He moves quickly between open spaces, with one weapon straight ahead and the other angled down each aisle. Stevens is six foot and bristling with genetically engineered muscles. Yet, even with all the tinkering, he's still pure blood.

Before the two men can close on us, Stevens finds one and fires, moving before the assassin can retaliate.

"Hermes, to your right, closing fast," Natasha says.

I find a shadow near the storefront to hide in. As the man creeps past me, I grab his shoulder. He turns too late. The shadow swallows him, and we take a short trip to the checkout.

130

"The first half-dozen trips are the hardest," I say, taking his weapon while he throws up in his helmet.

"Normally, I don't use guns. They're too loud," I say before shooting him in the back of the kneecap. His armor holds, so I shoot the same spot again. This time, it goes through his knee, bounces off the armor in front, and rattles inside his leg until the kinetic energy is spent and the bullet stops. He crumples to the floor. This time, I search for the assassin and find a knife strapped to his boot. I take it.

"Hermes, two more rides are coming in hot."

A barrage of bullets comes through broken windows while I dive for cover.

With bullets coming in through the front and Stevens in a gunfight to my left, I head right where no bullets fly

131

overhead. In the seasonal section are plastic pumpkins with motion sensors that laugh as you pass. I turn them on and keep moving. I know the assassins are behind me. I can feel them. I head back to the ceiling hole where moonlight pours through. I skulk into a shadow and inspect the knife. Nice blade. Its stiletto point is designed to punch through spider silk armor. A pumpkin laughs behind me, and I find a place to hide.

Soon, footsteps approach—two large men, if the loud clomping is any indication.

"Hermes, I can speed us up so you can take both out."

I shake my head. Since Natasha has rewired my nervous system, I'm capable of extra-fast short bursts of activity, but it tires me out for days. Instead, I wait for them to pass, step out of the shadow, stab one man in the thigh and step back inside. A spray of bullets hits empty air. I'm already several feet ahead of them. The noise attracts Steven's attention, and he shoots one in the calf muscle. I join Stevens and point to the ceiling. I take his arm and let the void disassemble our bodies. We reform on the roof. Sporadic gunfire echoes below as they shoot at phantoms. Eventually, they give up, get on their bikes, and leave.

I shift us back to ground level, and we head to the loading dock exit. A baleful whine sounds from beneath the steps. I stare into the shadow and glimpse a pair of red eyes. A scaleless hellhound, about the size of an Australian shepherd and weighing in at around 60 pounds, crouches in the darkness. She is surrounded by five pups, one significantly smaller than the others. Mom picks the runt up by the scruff of his neck and crawls toward me, her belly almost brushing the ground. Her eyes search mine, and she must find something pleasing in my expression because she places the pup at my feet. When I pick him up, the hound suckles my finger.

"I'll take care of him," I promise her.

She snorts an acknowledgment, then returns to her waiting brood. With a puppy cradled in my arms, we continue to Troll Town. "I hope you like cow's milk," I tell the pup. "Trolls make a rotting fish paste they consider a delicacy but refuse to drink goat milk because it's too gamey."

The red glow of Troll Town lights on the horizon lifts my mood.

Chapter Seven

It's 5 AM, and the sun will rise over Sacramento Estuary soon. The bats are heading home. Birds are warming up for their morning chorus.

Pam sits in her armored houseboat, drinking coffee and enjoying the show. The birds turn up the volume, and Big Mama Croc crawls out of her lagoon, hunting for breakfast. Pam's name for the 30-foot-long sacrodile is Katrina.

Katrina isn't fond of sharing her lagoon with a houseboat. Thankfully, the inch-thick, high-strength aluminum alloy defends the hull from her teeth and tail bashing. It took a few weeks for her to give up. The houseboat has been parked for a year, and Kiwi vines have colonized most of its surface. The metal bug screen keeps the vines off the deck.

Like her father, Pam loves being out on the water. It's her home. She patrols the estuary until she and Kim run out of supplies and have to head back to Ceres for more. Last year, they killed the pirates on the north side of the Bayou. Kim really likes shooting 50-caliber rounds. She says it's her *raison d'être*.

Pam returned from Vegas two weeks earlier, glad she and Hermes finally have closure. She and Jessie are a couple. It feels right. They've known each other for years, and there's a comfort in being around him, unlike Hermes, who is as unpredictable as he is entertaining.

"You boned him," Kim says. "Got on top and ground the poor boy into a paste."

Pam takes a deep breath and lets out a loud sigh.

Kim offers a smug smile and saunters toward the cabin. "Yes, yes, God, yes!" she yells, slamming her hips against the doorframe. Kim pauses to glance at Pam. "For a gal that speaks a dozen languages, you got a small sex vocabulary."

Pam stares at her coffee. "Of course, that's a secret."

Kim puts her hands on her hips. "Me? I'm a paragon of secrecy."

"I do not think that word means what you think it means."

"Really, because Hermes called you a paragon of femininity."

Pam glances at her friend. "Oh?"

"I've been rattling Hermes for days, trying to get him to crack. All he said was you were a 'paragon of femininity.'"

Pam smiles. "Paragon means a person or thing regarded as a perfect example of a particular quality. Hermes used the word correctly. However, you are not a paragon of secrecy."

"I can keep a secret. Maggie can't. And if I have a secret, Maggie knows. She'll ask questions. I don't answer them, but she always figures it out. So, it's only a matter of time."

"I'll talk to Maggie." Pam changes the subject. "Ready for a snake hunt?"

Anyone can make a designer monster with ten thousand credits and a basement. The anaconda genetic code is well known, and there are YouTube channels that teach monster-making. But someone has been creative, and the

30-foot serpent Pam's been asked to hunt is armored and spits hallucinogens. Its favorite tactic is to rise up and smash houseboats.

Kim and Pam eat hard-boiled eggs on toast while the artificial intelligence in Pam's Long-Range Interceptor warms up the diesel engine. It's a 35-foot rigid inflatable boat. Kevlar fibers give it a light armor rating.

It's tied next to the houseboat, which is a double-decker, and almost 2,000 square feet. Pam checks the Interceptor while Kim unties the rope. When Kim finishes and closes the door, the diesel engine's roar is muffled to a purr.

A typical fast attack craft is made of aluminum and designed for the ocean. They typically have a draft, the depth they can operate in, of 24 inches.

With its lighter weight, Pam's craft needs only 14 inches.

Carefully, Pam navigates the boat out of the lagoon and into a channel that meanders along the coast. It's another glorious day on the water. The summer solstice is only weeks away, and daily mountain thunderstorms keep the channels full. A male sacrodile makes a big splash with his tail. Pam gives him a wide berth. Their eyes meet as they pass.

When she spots a houseboat, she slows down. When the boats are a few meters apart, she reverses the jets, and the Interceptor stops. Kim opens the hatch, and a blue elf waves at them, wearing a straw hat. It's Callan.

"Did you find her?" Pam asks.

The elf nods and grins. "Oh yeah, Alva and Mike were out on patrol when Alva stumbled over the top of the snake in the tall grass. It spat in Alva's eyes, and suddenly, she was in love. Would've walked right into the snake's mouth if Mike didn't pull her away."

"Is Alva okay?"

"Yeah," Callan says. "Mike helped clean her up but got some on his hands and rubbed it in his eye. The two of them are in love and tripping balls."

Pam smiles. "Where's the snake now?"

"Mike emptied a clip from his M14, and it slithered back into the water. He thinks a couple of rounds got through its armored scales."

"This is going to be fun," Kim says.

"Let everyone know we're on our way."

"Roger that, Marshal," Callan says and tips his hat.

Pam maneuvers the Interceptor back into the channel while Callan taps on a tablet computer Hermes made with a 3D printer. It has a built-in camera and AM radio. There are four layers. The first is a hard plastic waterproof shell inside which the photovoltaic cells are printed. Inside another layer of plastic, there's an 11-foot antenna that picks up the local 90 MHz radio station, KRICE, and a backup satellite connection. Despite all this hardware, they're light enough to float on fresh water.

The radio station uses carrier waves to send text messages because microwaves don't travel well through the dense foliage in the Bayou. When the length of the wave is smaller than the dimensions of the obstacle it faces, it bounces back. However, it diffracts or bends when the wave is larger than the obstacle. Ceres' new FM station broadcasts at 90 MHz; its wavelength is eleven feet wider than the indigenous tree trunks.

Pam spots an airboat parked on a sandbar and stops.

A dwarf in a cowboy hat points to the east. "Bessy is in the dark water licking her wounds. She's pissed."

Kim climbs the ladder to the crow's nest in light armor and a helmet. Pam puts on her helmet and checks her Kevlar life vest. She steers the boat into the middle of the channel and proceeds slowly. In a few minutes, the channel narrows and deepens. Then, finally, it opens into a clearing surrounded by Cyprus trees. It's almost nine am, and half the lagoon is shrouded in shadow. Something big bumps into the ship, and she guns the throttle to full. Kim shoots into the water.

On the starboard side, Pam sees the head of a snake. A column of green, six feet in diameter, rises from the water. Kim keeps firing. Fifty-caliber rounds punch through the snake's armor, and thick blood oozes from multiple wounds.

When the snake reaches its full height, it falls toward the Interceptor, crashing into the stern.

The serpent's mass drags the stern underwater. Kim keeps firing while the cabin fills with water and spent shells.

Before the engine compartment can fill up, the Interceptor slides from under the snake's coils and bobs to the surface. Pam turns on the bilge pump and leaves the lagoon. When they are clear by a hundred yards, she turns the boat around and waits for the pump to clean the cabin of water. Kim swears in Japanese while she clears her weapon.

Within ten minutes, the cabin is dry.

"You ready?" Pam asks.

Kim cocks the 50-caliber weapon. "Let's see if puppy got any more of that weak ass shit left."

They head back to the lagoon, where turbid water hides the anaconda from sight. Suddenly, the serpent slams down amidship, and the Interceptor is lifted out of the water. It lands on its side. The serpent bites the machine gun, ripping it from its mounts.

Kim slides down onto the deck and grabs an M14. As the Interceptor rights itself, the snake rams its armored head against the boat. The vessel rolls three times and stops in a grove of cattails. The air is filled with cotton. The boat lists 30 degrees in the marshland.

145

It's eerily quiet after all the gunfire and engine noise. Pam grabs her service pistol, lowers the visor on her helmet and slides into the water. Kim passes an M16 to Pam, keeping her M14 ready, then splashes down. As rustling noises surround them, Pam questions the wisdom of her decision to leave the boat.

The giant snake rises above the reeds and strikes at the boat's exhaust, perhaps attracted by the heat. It doesn't see the women, so they take the opportunity to shoot the monster in the eye. The serpent spits, enraged. They keep firing at its head, and it wobbles. After its next strike, it slowly recovers, allowing Kim to climb on top and stab its other eye with a trench knife. It tries to shake her off, but Kim clings to a horn and keeps stabbing and swearing, stabbing and swearing, stabbing and swearing, until finally, the dying snake stops writhing in agony and is still. It takes almost an hour.

"Well, that's that," Kim says.

"Not quite. Now we do an autopsy to see its stomach contents."

With the help of Callen and Mathol, they haul the serpent to a sandy spot by the water's edge and see through its relatively soft underbelly. Pam has to swallow an unexpected bout of nausea before taking photos. It looks as though its diet was mainly fish and smaller crocs, but they find the remains of a few people. Kim retrieves boat keys and a wedding ring, and then Callen and Mathol remove what is left of the bodies and put them in plastic bags.

Finally, Kim cuts out its venom sacks and stores them in her cooler. "That should put a little spice in the love life."

More people arrive and help pull the boat back into the water. There are dents all along the aluminum frame. When the Interceptor is ready, they wave goodbye and return to Ceres.

Kim puts her hand on Pam's shoulder. "Life just doesn't get better than this."

Pam allows herself a small smile. "Yes, this is a good life."

Chapter Eight

I make the final adjustments to Stevens' mustache. I've darkened his complexion, changed his eye color with contacts, and added a wig.

He studies himself in a mirror. "How about that? I look like Raoul."

Today, I'm Samuel Pérez, a 72-year-old retired CEO. The actual Mr. Pérez is currently in Florida and has a limp, so I've been practicing walking with a cane for days. I made it on my 3D printer. It's titanium alloy coated in a wood-effect plastic. Only the bottom and top spheres look like metal.

I dress in spider silk, a vest, a white shirt, and a black suit that's one size too big to make it look like I've recently lost weight. I set the skin augment to a slightly pale face and add age spots to my hands. While I'm fussing with my grey wig, Stevens checks out my kitchen.

He opens the fridge. "What's in the big Tupperware?"

"Grrrrr," Krypto replies.

Krypto is the hellhound puppy I adopted. The runt. Like all hellhounds, he has red eyes and black fur, so dark that he's hard to see at night except for his eyes and claws.

Stevens opens the box. "It's a dead weasel."

Krypto rises from his spot under my feet and stalks over to the fridge. He glares at Stevens until the box is restored to its rightful place.

150

"If I throw it away, Krypto shits in my shoes. Lines them all up and adds a little bit in each one."

Stevens chuckles. He walks around and inspects my furniture. "What's with all the bamboo?"

"I like bamboo," I say.

Natasha interrupts. *"Because it's cheap."*

Natasha fills the six-foot screen on my living room wall. She's wearing a brown pantsuit, and her hair is tight bun.

I finish adjusting my wig and walk into the kitchen. I pull the drawer open with a single finger. "Did you hear that?" I don't wait for Stevens to answer. "Neither did I."

Stevens plays with my silverware drawer. "I see your point, but it still looks cheap."

Natasha gives me an I-told-you-so look.

I grab my cane and head outside to clear my head and get into character. Before long, a four-door compact car pulls up. It's a diesel. The seaweed farms off the coast produce enough cheap oil to ensure compact diesels remain popular.

Stevens gets in the front and puts the seat all the way back, leaving me no legroom. I sit with my feet on the bench seat.

In ten minutes, we're at the front gate and join a caravan of eight cars heading to Frisco. We travel in packs to deter the bandits that patrol the roads. We drive silently even though banter is an excellent way to release nervous energy before a job. Today is different because it's my first paid acting job, or it will be if we're successful. My only weapon is the cane. Stevens has plastic knuckles with the same density as human flesh that scanners can't detect.

Forty-five minutes later, we approach the front gate of Frisco. A guard checks our IDs and waves us through. Another fifteen minutes and we drive into a garage and park in a camera blind spot next to a full-sized sedan.

We switch cars and drivers. I tuck my cane between my legs and settle in the back seat while Stevens closes my door. Once Stevens is inside, the driver heads down the ramp, and we merge into traffic. A few minutes later, he stops in front of Northwest Bank.

"It's show time. You good?"

Stevens gives a tight nod.

"You're going to do fine. Follow my lead and say nothing, Raoul."

He opens the door. "Next time, I get to pick my street name."

Stevens helps me out of the car and then hands me the cane. I use it to walk a dozen steps to the entrance. Stevens opens the door, and we approach the counter. I show the young woman my Samuel Pérez ID and safety deposit key.

The first woman leads me to another, a mutant with large eyes in her mid-thirties. There's a retinal scanner on her desk. She scrutinizes my ID before handing it back. Her nametag says, Nancy.

"Mr. Pérez, please place your chin on the rest."

A red laser scans my cyber eyes, altered to match Samuel's.

"Thank you, sir, and now, if I can see your signature."

"*Darling, allow me,*" Natasha takes control of my hand and signs Pérez's name. She's perfect, as usual.

"Follow me, please," Nancy says.

I hide my smile and raise my hand. "Raoul."

Stevens looks at me, then realizes I'm talking to him. He takes my hand and helps me to my feet. I lean on my cane and follow Nancy to the back, where they keep the safety deposit boxes. She uses a key to open the metal gate, and we walk through.

I follow slowly, leaning on my cane and ensuring my hand is curled as if my movements are limited post-stroke. I love acting. I should do more jobs like this.

Nancy stops at the box and waits for me to catch up. "I'll give you some privacy," she says, walking away.

I take the safety deposit box key out of my pocket and try to insert it into the lock. In case we're still being watched, I make my hand tremble and give the key to Raoul. He opens the box and slides the drawer out.

"*The writing is German. They're bearer bonds, and each is half a million credits,*" Natasha tells me.

"Raoul, be a good boy and empty the box."

Stevens retrieves a shopping bag inside his jacket pocket and stuffs it with bonds. We leave the room and wait while Nancy locks the gate behind us. We are halfway to the exit when two security guards block our way.

"Mr. Pérez, you know you can't take anything out unless I get the call. Please come with—"

Stevens swings the shopping bag wide as a distraction and slams the plastic knuckles into the guard's chin. He drops to the ground. The second guard turns to face Stevens, and I strike my cane against the back of his knees. The guard grunts and falls to the floor.

Exit time. We run outside, where two men on motorcycles wait at the curb. A quick hop on the back of the bikes, and we lurch forward just as a security man emerges, holding a taser. We take the first left and stay in the alleys. Minutes later, we are back at the parking garage. A nondescript car waits at the exit with its engine turning over and its windows rolled down. Stevens tosses the bearer bonds onto the back seat. Rather than enter the garage, we head downhill along a one-way alley for a few blocks and stop behind a mini-diesel. We get off the bikes and into the car. I pull a trash bag from my vest pocket, and Stevens hands me his wig.

"That was an amazing rush." He gives me his jacket next. "I see the attraction of your line of work."

I stuff his clothes in the trash bag. "We're not done yet. At the next light, take out your contacts and wipe off the makeup." I unscrew my cane and hide it under the seat.

After removing my jacket and pants and putting them in the trash bag, I change into jeans, a t-shirt, and training shoes. "Driver, stop at a burn barrel."

I help Stevens remove his makeup and put the wet wipes in the trash bag. The driver spots a burn barrel with a man feeding the fire and stops mid-block. I walk over, hand the man a silver dime, and put our trash inside the barrel. I return to the car, and we move before the door shuts.

I breathe a sigh of relief. "Now, I feel better." I check my virtual watch. "From start to finish—twenty minutes."

"Wow, it felt like hours," Stevens says.

"Usually, something goes wrong, and I have to wing it. It seems wrong that everything went right."

"That's because we're part of a team with highly trained people looking after us."

I lean back in the seat. "Yeah, but I miss being chased."

Steven chuckles.

Ten minutes later, we exit Frisco with another caravan. In less than an hour, I'm home and waving goodbye to Stevens and our driver.

Krypto runs over and greets me. Having someone happy to see you when you get home isn't too shabby.

Chapter Nine

Pam sits on the toilet and prays. "God, Jesus, Allah, Buddha, Ahura Mazda, and to all gods of light, please, please, may the answer be NO."

She opens her eyes and glares at the stick—two bright, bold lines. Pregnant. Of course, she is. Her boobs are like bullets inside the spider silk mesh. By the timing, she's certain it's Hermes'. Whoever coined what happens in Vegas stays in Vegas is a bald-faced liar. The combination of danger, alcohol and romance triggered early ovulation.

She will keep the baby. Pam loves children. At last count, she has twenty.

She pats her belly. "You are twenty-one."

*   *   *

On the water, her problems melt away. Pam and Kim patrol the channels. It's mid-July, and the Bayou is overflowing with life. The Interceptor cruises at a fuel-saving 10 knots. A seven-foot sturgeon follows the boat, looking for any shellfish the jets might churn up from the silty bottom.

Kim walks up behind and massages her shoulders. "You tell Jessie?"

"I only found out this morning, and he's at the Navy base for training."

"So, Spooky slipped one past the goalpost."

Pam nods. "That he did."

Kim's fingers move upward and massage her neck. Tactful for once, she says nothing.

"Don't you have some witty and vulgar remark?"

"Usually, I'd pass comment on the elephant in the room that everyone is pretending isn't there. But that's an eleph—" Kim stiffens.

"Less pressure," Pam yelps.

Kim releases her grip and points to the shore. "I hear people-buzz."

No boats are visible, so Pam turns on the Interceptor's active camouflage. There is a silt deposit covered in blackberries ahead. Pam moors the boat on the opposite side and switches off the engine. When her ears adjust to the quiet, she recognizes the faint sound of a diesel engine. They're on the north side of the Bayou. A wildlife sanctuary. There shouldn't be any cars or trucks

162

for miles. Kim and Pam put on thorn-proof Kevlar body suits. The fabric has active camouflage and is slicker than human skin. They pull helmets with built-in microphones over their hair. Finally, they grab their nine-millimeter service pistols and a hand-held waterproof video camera with a zoom lens. Kim, never one to be caught underdressed, takes an M16.

The channel is 160-feet wide. Kim crosses first while Pam covers her position. Once she's safely hidden, Pam swims the distance underwater. Pam's augments include an extra lens for each eye, so she has great underwater vision and flaps that close off her nose and ears while swimming. She's been known to quip that she's part mermaid. This far upstream, the water is like a crystal. Kim's legs and the embankment get clearer as she closes in.

When Pam reaches the shore, the engine noise is pronounced. She and Kim slip out of the water and clamber under Cypress trees. Using the trees as cover, they carefully move toward the noise. Men are feeding dead wood to a chipper. A bobcat with a loader on front picks up a pile of woodchips and makes a path through the thicket. Pam records everything.

The women maneuver through the trees and around the construction, taking videos from every angle. Another woman in a cargo all-terrain vehicle or CATV is typing into a satellite phone. Pam zooms in and gets a close-up of her face. Then Kim and Pam circle back and return to the Interceptor. They change into dry clothes and head back to Ceres.

"A road made of wood chips won't last more than a few months," Kim says.

Pam guides the boat onto the main channel. "You wouldn't be able to transport anything heavy."

"And it won't hold up to much traffic. Maybe two hundred light infantry and their gear on ATVs, max."

Pam nods. "Yup. This is big, too big to broadcast over the airwaves."

Kim squeezes Pam's shoulder. "Roger that."

Chapter Ten

I am one of a dozen people whom Colonel James truly trusts. All of us are sitting around his conference room table. Major Hayes is seated on the colonel's right. Sargent Conrad is to his left.

The colonel leans back in his chair and puts his hands behind his head. "I have in my possession eight million in bearer bonds."

"We could pay off the water tower and photovoltaic loans and still have enough money to invest in a sewage treatment plant," Garry Rents says.

"I don't think so," I reply. My gut is ringing alarm bells. "The junkies and homeless have disappeared from Frisco, and missing person reports have tripled statewide. Something's up. I recommend we use the money to buy our rice harvest and have the trolls hide it in the Bayou."

"A proposal is on the table to use the money to purchase Ceres' rice. Is there a second?"

"Second," John Crandall replies.

"I call for a vote. All in favor say 'Aye.'"

Since everyone in the room is a rice farmer, everyone votes for my plan.

"The motion is carried unanimously," the colonel says, bangs his gavel. "Next item of business is Marshall Fields' report."

Pam stands up. "Someone is constructing an all-terrain-vehicles road

167

using wood chips. They are clearing thicket on the north side of the Bayou, but they're being careful not to cut down trees that could expose their efforts."

"Baron's building a road to our back door!" Garry says. Garry Rents is the youngest of the bio-wars veterans present. His hair is grey only on the sides.

"That probably means he's planned something bigger for our front door," I say.

"Exactly," the colonel says. "Let's quietly evacuate anyone who wants to leave. Meanwhile, we'll continue our summer activities and act like business as usual." He changes the subject. "The next item of business is the thorium reactors, Sargent Clark."

Marion Clark stands up. "We have three mini-reactors with a one-hundred-kilowatt rating. Hermes has one for his boat, Colonel Baker for his, and the third will power the mobile base camp."

"Why thorium reactors?" Garry asks.

"Thorium fission reactions don't get as hot as uranium. These reactors are made to easily withstand the reaction temperatures. There is no risk of meltdowns. Plus, the fission by-products take hundreds rather than the thousands of years of a uranium reactor." Marion sits.

Colonel James nods. "Thank you, Sargent Clark. Does anyone have any other business?"

"Yes," I hold up a playing card. "I printed two hundred radio wave repeaters that look like cards. On one side, there's a photovoltaic cell. The other has a radio receiver, transmitter and antenna embedded. They can

169

receive and transmit encrypted text messages to the next receiver in the sequence and have a range of 1,300 feet. If we get people to hang them on the sunny side of creeks and channels, they will form a secure communications network."

"I have contacts in the Bayou," Pam says.

I smile. "Thanks."

"That's very ingenious, Hermes. Anyone else?" Colonel James asks.

The room is quiet. I sit with my hands in my lap, grinning, until it dawns on me that the colonel can be a condescending bastard at times.

"Dismissed."

Everyone leaves except me.

"What's on your mind?" the colonel asks.

"I'm having problems with microwaves. The wireless mic in my goggles burns my ears. An augment is available that interlaces conductive wires into a mesh that transmits and receives. It distributes the signal rather than concentrating it near the ear canal. I discussed it with my doctor, and she says I need a recommendation from my commanding officer."

He smiles and puts his hand on my shoulder. "I see. And so, who is your commanding officer?"

I cringe. "You're not going to make me say it."

"I insist."

"You are, C-Colonel Ja-ja-ames," I stutter.

"That wasn't too painful. Maybe, one day, you'll even manage to call me Colonel Baker. It's only one extra syllable."

Don't count on it, I think. He grins. If I didn't know better, I might believe he read my mind.

After an excruciatingly long dramatic pause, he continues. "I'll pass on my recommendation. Anything else?"

I walk away. "Oh God, I feel dirty; I need a shower."

"Drama Queen," he says.

"The things I put up with," I mumble.

Chapter Eleven

I'm sitting on a barstool with tassels. After my third drink, I notice Shirley Temple sitting next to me. This time, she's wearing a black dress that reaches her knees and gloves up to her elbows.

"What's your name?" I ask.

"Brigette, I was a Flapper in my day."

"Yeah, I do some flying."

Brigette giggles.

"Mom says you're a yegg. Do you use soup to crack your egg or spin the wheel of fortune?"

"Huh?"

"You a safecracker?"

"I deny all allegations."

She snorts. "Yeah, the bulls give me the heebie-jeebies." Brigette kicks my leg lightly. "That's why you keep your getaway sticks in top shape."

I nod. "It's all about cardio."

"I drank and smoked too much, and consumption got me. I don't mind death, but I do mind dying."

"If I was dying of TB, I'd go to Vegas, rent a Lamborghini, and take an insurance company with me."

Brigette looks at me, and her eyes narrow. "I like the way you think." She holds up her glass. "Hey Rick, we need more of this giggle water."

Bogart comes over and pours our drinks. The place is hopping and festive, so he has no time to chat.

Then suddenly, I understand. "You're my daughter."

174

Brigette raises her glass.

I hold up my glass and clink it against hers. "See you on the other side."

"See you on the flip."

* * *

I wake at nine am, which is early for me. I think about the *Casablanca* dream while I get dressed. It's still vivid, so I tell Natasha the details.

I work through my morning routine: breakfast, check the news, and jog with Krypto.

My hellhound is the town's hero: hanging out by chicken coops and hunting weasels every night. He brings home a half-eaten weasel once a week, and I tell him he's a good boy.

I clean the house until a delivery van arrives. I didn't want to print a few

175

thousand LEDs, so I ordered them. Since they are inexpensive, I made them with bells and whistles to jack up the price per unit. They're food-grade plastic spheres the size of marbles with graphene capacitors and ultra-efficient diodes. The gizmo even comes with a photovoltaic to shut off during daylight. With all the extras, they cost ten cents apiece. The minimum order was 20,000 credits.

I open the empty bay where I stored my diesel Humvee before I moved it to the Navy base for (hopefully) safekeeping. Twenty boxes with 10,000 LEDs are unloaded. Each box contains a different color. I tip the driver a silver dollar. He compliments my chrome front door.

Tomorrow, I'm expecting a delivery of microwave and radio wave repeaters. They're also the size of marbles with nylon cords attached. These signal repeaters can be tied to trees or float on water.

A quick lunch, then back to work. At least my ears no longer overheat while I'm using the wireless. The skull has too many openings for microwaves to enter, and my infrared goggles and video glasses pump out microwaves to stay connected to the internet. I made a jacket to act as an antenna, but it takes time to plug in the fiber optic line, and it's prone to disconnect when running for my life. But my new augment solves those problems. The doctor added metallic silver to the spider silk mesh woven into my skin. Now, it conducts electricity and acts as an antenna. Each of my limbs is assigned a zone and several subzones. For example, my calves and the top of my head emit microwaves, and my forearms are receivers. The video glasses relay the signals to Natasha. Since the glasses touch my skin, I can reduce the transmitter power by 100,000. Much better. I spend the afternoon modifying my goggles and video glasses. Krypto naps in the warmest spot of the garden, moving with the sun.

When my adjustments are complete, Natasha reminds me of the potluck, and I pick fresh leaves, tomatoes, peppers, and cucumber for the salad. Natasha and I make short work of chopping and then put everything into glass bowls with plastic lids. Hands full of food, I push the front door button with my foot. Krypto bolts out and jumps into my quarter-ton pickup bed. I put the plastic bowls on the passenger seat. It's mid-August, and rice is a few weeks from harvest. Scatterings of dry leaves lie near a few tree trunks. I climb into the electric truck and head out. Mom and Dad's home is nestled against the foothills on the other side of town. I drive through the town center, take a right onto Baker Road and drive west. In ten minutes, we pass Colonel James' home. A few miles further north, my parents grow 160 acres of hemp. I turn into their driveway. They built the house to take advantage of the shade of the mature native oaks that dominate this section of the hill. I park beside Pam's pickup. Nowadays, everyone drives an electric quarter-ton pickup with batteries in the back. I like to think I started the trend.

I skirt the one-story farmhouse and enter their backyard. I put the salad on the serving table. The gang's all here: Kim, Maggie, Pam and Jessie. Krypto sniffs under the table and finds something to eat. Mom hugs me, and we join the group, standing in the shade. Everyone looks at me. My eyes meet Pam's, and I smile. She returns my smile and takes a step toward me. Everyone stops talking.

"Hermes, I'm pregnant; it's your child."

I remember my dream, and everything makes sense. "Her name is Brigette."

Then bam. Pam slaps me. "It's not okay to be spooky right now." She is on the verge of tears.

I nod. "Okay. Sorry."

"Hey Conrad," Stevens says, bitch-slapping me to the ground. Fireflies dance around the edges of my vision. "That's for getting my girlfriend pregnant."

I try to think up something clever to say while I get up.

Dad kicks me in the ass, and I fall forward. Krypto uses this opportunity to attack my shoe. First, he pulls it off and runs. Then, he swings his head back and forth, slamming my shoe against the ground while growling. The savagery of Krypto's attack has everyone laughing, which only encourages his performance. He returns my soggy, part-mauled shoe when his point has been made.

Kim helps me to my feet and then punches my shoulder. "That's for making me keep a secret."

"How did you manage? I know how hard it is for you not to blurt out whatever's on your mind."

Kim puts her hand on my shoulder, and we get in line for food. Everyone else avoids me except Mom.

She brings her lawn chair close to mine. "I knew it. Pam returned from Vegas and couldn't look me in the eye."

I nod and eat. Mom is so happy she's bubbling. I finish my plate but leave plenty of meat on the ribs. I put the plate down, and Krypto swallows the bones whole and then begs for more.

"So, what about you? You haven't said a word."

"That's because I'm eating," I say.

"Tell me, what are you thinking?"

To build tension, I take a slow sip of my tea. "I've had dreams about Brigette. I think she got Dad's DARPA genes."

"About one in three inherent the strength and stamina gene. It's partially active with you but combined with Pam's genetic engineering, who knows what your child will be able to do. How do you feel about becoming a father? You've never talked about kids."

"That's because I didn't think I'd ever get laid again."

Mom chuckles and then stares at me until I continue.

"I've been smitten with Pam since I first laid eyes on her. But I said or did the wrong thing every time we interacted."

Mom nods.

"I get it. We're not a couple. We're too different. Pam is my friend and the mother of my child, but that's the beginning and end of our relationship. I wish it could be different, but..." I shrug. "So, I guess what I feel is peace."

"I know what you mean. I have a grandchild on the way, and all is well."

Chapter Twelve

Colonel James is alone in his conference room. The video screen is split between Major Hayes and the colonel. Kim and I are at my house.

"We found the missing homeless. They joined the New Life Ministry and are cleaning up the burnt section of Frisco," Major Hayes reports.

I interrupt. "Excuse me. Are you saying that junkies, the mentally ill, and other people who have long given up on life, are picking up trash?"

"Apparently, yes."

"Huh," Kim and I say together. Kim has lived on the streets and knows better than any of us how strange that sounds.

"There's a new preacher in town, Reverend Jim. Our intelligence suggests he uses a psionic device to influence the crowd," Colonel Baker says. "Kim, Hermes, I want you two to check it out."

I grin, delighted. "I'm always up for a night out on the town."

*   *   *

So, Kim and I are going to Frisco to check out a preacher who convinced the city's down-and-outs to pick up trash. With John as our driver, we join a caravan.

Kim is riding shotgun. She unclips her seat belt and turns to face me. "You know why Vanya won't fuck you anymore?"

"Zombie Ziggy Grave Dust."

185

"What were you thinking?"

"Vanya's a horror fan. She said she wanted to see my zombie. So, I bought some hemp bails and a headstone, spread some straw and dirt, set up a few laser holograms and waited for the next full moon."

John adjusts his rearview mirror to look at me. He never says anything. He doesn't have to with his expressive eyebrows and smirking mouth.

"I rose from the grave with my holographic zombie dancers, and Vanya screamed bloody murder."

"You know why?"

"Too realistic?"

"When you do that mist and fog thing, it sucks the heat out of the air, and your skin glows in black light."

"It looks electric blue to me," John says. "Like the sheen on an oil slick."

186

"Not everyone can see it," Kim says. "But Vanya saw it really well."

"Oh."

"So, you might want to retire Zombie Ziggy Grave Dust if you ever want to get laid again."

John chuckles and slows down for the main gate into Frisco.

Frisco is divided by the Bay Bridge. About a third of North Frisco burned to the water line. With garbage pickup too dangerous after the virus riots, residents dumped their trash in the burned section. Now, the debris has been cleared, and the only traces are a few glittery patches of glass shards that brighten the pavement. We drive around the edges of the burnt section to get the lay of the land. Then, John pulls into a parking garage a few blocks away.

Kim and I put our backpacks on a walk down the ramp and into the city.

187

The whiff of burning garbage and the bark of dogs make us feel nostalgic.

"Honey, I'm home," I say out loud.

"I don't miss the street hustle one bit."

We're near the boundary between retail stores and apartments. In five blocks, we're at the edge of the burnt section. The toasted cars have been towed away, and the trash is missing. We continue toward the water's edge.

According to Reverend Jim's website, he has a sermon daily at seven p.m. That's in twenty minutes. A double-decker houseboat lit up with LEDs bobs on the water. A large gathering, maybe a thousand, watch from the shore. This area was a park with a trail meandering around the water. Jumbo screens are set up in the parking lot.

People sit on blankets in the grassy areas. Spotting an empty space, we do the same. Long-fingered mutants hand out bottles of water to everyone while festive music plays. Ten minutes later, a shiny bald man steps out onto the roof of the houseboat and warms up the crowd by telling them how great a job they've done cleaning up. Then Reverend Jim takes the stage. He talks slowly and deliberately. His mesmerizing eyes fill the TV screen.

"I know you hurt. The world has rejected and forgotten you. Why? You only want what everyone else has. Why should you get less? Let me give you a hint. It's not because of bad karma. It's not because you're lazy, stupid, or any other excuse the man gives you. You can't succeed because the world robs you blind."

189

He pauses for effect. I see the crowd nod their agreement.

"Your birth certificate is your death certificate. License fees tax the food you eat and, if you let them, the air you breathe. Who is our enemy? It's always the same: the people with armies. They make the laws, not you."

A grumble spreads through the crowd. The emotion is thick; I can taste it. The reverend raises a pint-sized water bottle, and everyone raises theirs, including Kim.

"Drink, drink in new life. Drink the power to defeat our enemies." He drinks.

I glance at Kim. The bottle is at her lips. I grab her hand, and the water spills on the blanket. I stand up and pull her away. After a dozen hasty steps, Kim revives.

"Fuck, those big screens were pumping out something that got in my head."

A middle-aged man with a big belly and a nightstick clipped to his belt approaches. "You didn't drink your water. If you want to leave, you'll drink that right now."

I get the pint bottle from my vest pocket and put it between my thighs. "Why don't you suck on it," I say, thrusting my hips.

He unclips the club from his belt. Before I can kick him in the balls, Kim punches him in the temple. Her muscle and bone augments make her twice as strong as an average man. The guard's head rocks back and forth from the impact. He sways for ten seconds while I visualize cartoon birds flying around his head, and then he falls hard on the asphalt. Kim slams her boot into his

191

nose to ensure he stays down, then grabs his nightstick.

We cover a dozen steps before more guards show up.

In one motion, I remove my backpack, swing it at the closest man and retrieve my baton. With a flick of the wrist, it extends. While he bats my pack away, I swat the back of his knees twice.

Kim ditches her pack and closes in on the next guard. A guard raises his nightstick, and Kim grabs his arm and smashes his nose flat with her forehead. The ferocity of her attack makes the other guards think twice, and we use the opportunity to sprint away.

After forty meters, the pack of out-of-shape guards huff and puff to a stop. If I was filming a Frisco Nights webcast, this would be the point when I would shake my dick and shout obscenities to encourage the chase. I should have brought a camera. Instead, we slow to a fast-paced walk.

Kim screws on the silencer to her tech-9. We reach the edge of the burn section before a police cruiser stops, and a cop starts to get out.

Kim rushes the man while he's partly inside the vehicle and points her gun at his crotch. "You want these hollow point bullets shredding your boys?"

"Ma'am, you don't want to do that," he says then looks at me.

I pull on my thieving gloves. "Sorry, but she doesn't listen to me. You're on your own." I remove the keys from the ignition and open the trunk.

Kim takes his gun.

"Ma'am, you really don't want to do that."

"You're wrong. I've always wanted to do this. It's actually a fantasy of mine," Kim says, slamming his head against the door's rim.

When her hands move lower, I can't tell whether Kim is frisking or molesting him. Probably both. She cuffs him and then shoves the cop into the trunk. Kim blows him a kiss before lowering the decklid.

"TTFN, or ta-ta for now," I say.

I put on my video glasses, and Natasha connects to the internet. It's effortless compared to fumbling for a fiber optic port behind my ear.

Kim leads the way into the commercial district. It's 7:30 p.m. and not quite dark. We pass a series of auto repair shops. An abandoned gas station with boarded-up windows has a bathroom in the back. I pick the lock, and Kim and I get in and close the door.

194

"Why are the cops after us?" Kim asks.

"It seems Reverend Jim and the police are buddies, or he's paying them." I take the water bottle out of a vest pocket. "My guess is they really want this back."

"Hermes," Natasha whispers. *"I informed the Colonel."*

Light from the crack under the door illuminates the bathroom. I check my virtual watch: twenty minutes until sunset. The light moves, and the sound of an engine subsides.

"There is an all-points bulletin for a man and woman meeting your descriptions," Natasha says.

I stare at my watch. Time is moving too slowly. "This doesn't feel right. Let's go."

I open the door, peek and listen. The way seems to be clear. Kim and I move quickly into the lengthening shadows. The back alleys are lined with cars waiting to be fixed. Kim kicks a lug nut, and it pings off a stack of axles. A drone shines a spotlight on us.

"Natasha, can you take care of this."

After a brief pause, the drone flies away at high speed and crashes into a wall. Kim and I jog in the opposite direction.

"Hermes," Natasha says. *"Colonel Baker has been monitoring police communications. They're tracking the water bottle."*

I find a recycling bin, extract a piece of aluminum foil, and wrap the bottle so no plastic is exposed. The makeshift Faraday cage will block GPS and RFI signals.

Kim and I keep moving north toward higher ground.

"*Hermes,*" Natasha says. "*Stop at the end of the alley. A woman on a motorcycle is coming. Hand her the water bottle.*"

In a few minutes, an electric bike stops. I step out of the shadows and give her the bottle. She tucks it inside her jacket, nods a salute, and drives away.

Kim and I cross the street and keep moving.

"Why take the bottle and not us?" Kim asks.

"Because two people on an electric bike are slow. If they're tracking the bottle, you want to be fast."

"Roger that," Kim says.

We stop at the intersection. It's a wide-open space, so we hide in the shadow of a semi-truck. Cold creeps over my skin, announcing sunset. I relax.

Kim taps my shoulder and points to the six-foot culvert under the road. The area is well-lit with red LEDs. I hold out my hand.

Kim takes it. "If I throw up, I'm punching you."

The web of shadows takes us in, and we exist without thought for a few seconds. Then my mind reforms enough to remember the pipe, and we stand beside it. I take Kim's hand and walk inside. There are a few inches of water at the bottom.

"Natasha, they're looking for two homeless people, so we need the change of clothes in the back seat of our getaway vehicle."

"On it," Natasha says.

Kim dry heaves a few times, then gives me a thumbs up, followed by the middle finger.

"There are dozens of drones looking for you," Natasha says. *"They're searching every car leaving Frisco."*

"Someone really wants their water bottle back," I say.

Soon, a large plastic bag drops a few yards away. I step out from the cover, grab the bag and rush back. Kim and I change into our going out-to-dinner clothes. Plan B is to stay in the city and act like a couple having a night out there. Still wearing our spider silk undergarments, we change quickly into designer jeans and shirts. Natasha changes my features and skin tone so I appear Hispanic. Kim lightens her skin a couple of shades, but it's still dark enough to disguise her stripes. I take her hand and shift back to the parted-out semi. Then we move to a location where I can see for three blocks. In a commercial area, two people on foot might look suspicious after dark. However, five blocks north, there's a restaurant and bar. We make another shift, wait a few minutes for Kim to catch her breath, then shift again. Across the street is a gas station. A few doors down, there's a clothing shop. I buy us fake leather jackets while a cop car cruises past. I love this part of the job, hiding in plain sight. I pay with cash, and we cross the street to a seafood restaurant where we get fish and chips with clam chowder and coleslaw. I take a mouthful of the chowder and make a face.

"What's wrong?" Kim asks.

"It's overcooked, the clams are chewy, and there's a hint of burn."

"I can't tell whether it's burnt, but yeah, chewy. The fish is crisp," Kim says, making a big crunch with her massive jaw.

I chuckle and continue eating.

"Wow, all the shifting cleared my head. Those screens were pumping out some toxic shit. It was trying to make a nest in my head."

"Yea, shadow walk is a sure cure for a hangover."

Kim changes the subject. "I know you fucked Pam, or more accurately, Pam fucked you."

I blush and look down.

"So, you don't have anything to say?"

"My evening with Pam is special, and no matter what I say, you're going to make some off-color comment."

"Cross my heart, hope to die, stick a needle in my eye. I'll keep my mouth shut."

"Pam is sensual, tactile, and very affectionate. I never felt that connected to a woman. And because of that

201

connection, I know we're not right for each other."

Kim smiles. "Pam touches everything before she eats it. For example, when she smells a peach, she holds it against her nose and gives a big sniff."

We wait while police cruisers pass by every ten minutes. I smile smugly.

"Darling, we have a plan. The police are looking for a couple, so Kim's ride will be out front in a few minutes."

I pay the bill with a silver dollar, walk outside, and a car pulls up to the curb. Kim and I hug, and she gets inside.

I walk down the street. "Natasha, how far is Troll Town from here?"

"As the crow flies, six miles, eight miles by road."

"Tell the Colonel I'll be at the *Hole in the Wall* restaurant getting rid of the taste of burnt chowder. Eight miles of shifting will work up an appetite."

"If Krypto smells food on you, he'll be pissed. Make sure you order a take-out."

"Roger that," I say and shift into the shadows.

Chapter Thirteen

The colonel is alone in his conference room. A large screen displays a dozen people's faces.

"The Navy hospital says the water bottle was filled with nanites designed to migrate to the brain and form an implant. These new models connect to the pleasure and addiction centers of the brain."

"So that's how you get junkies to pick up trash," Kim says.

"When do you think they will attack?" Sargent Conrad asks.

Colonel Baker leans back in his chair and puts his hands behind his head. "Baron will wait until the rice harvest is dried and put into our silos to maximize profit."

"So, any time after mid-October," Major Hayes says.

The colonel nods. "That's five weeks away. Effective immediately, we will evacuate all nonessential personnel."

Chapter Fourteen

Pam is five months pregnant. The Colonel has ordered her to stay on the boat. Vanya accompanies them while Pam and Kim cruise the Bayou.

Pam's meeting Maggie for coffee at ten. She drives away from the new subdivision where homes are on two-acre lots, the smallest lot size allowed without a sewage treatment plant. Any smaller and overcrowding could contaminate the groundwater and leach into fields.

She takes a left on Main Street. Halloween season starts on the first of October, and pumpkins and straw people are near every front door. It's the second week in October, and a third of Ceres has already left. Most are in guest housing on the Navy base. The remaining residents have added extra decorations to make it look like business as usual.

On the left is Maggie's. Pam parks out front and heads inside. Maggie waves. A few people sit at the counter. Pam is directed to a table on the covered patio. Maggie brings pumpkin muffins and coffee to her table. Three women arrive. Pam recognizes them all from the Broadmoor Country Club.

"Why, Pamela, you look absolutely radiant these days. I'm sure Jessie is thrilled. Not to pry, but the timing of your trip to Vegas and pregnancy is suggestive."

As the resident maliciously gossips, Sharron must know Hermes is the father. Maggie has known for months and can never keep a secret, especially not anything this huge. Pam refuses to rise to the bait. She will not be shamed by this coven of busybodies with no lives of their own. The only reason they're still in Ceres is because they're military wives.

Pam takes a deep breath and decides she'll give the women more than they bargained for. She'll take a leaf from Hermes' book and make it a memorable performance. "Hermes is the father."

It's incredible how silence descends so quickly. At Maggie's, the clank of dishes and conversations is a constant, but it's dead quiet when Pam makes her announcement. Like cockroaches, people appear out of nowhere after lights go out and circle the table. Pam takes a moment to butter her pumpkin muffin, add creamer to the coffee, and take a sip.

"If I tell the story once, you'll never ask me again. Agreed?"

The crowd nods, and a few people get out their cell phones and press record.

"I met up with Hermes in Vegas. He called himself Rick Savage and dressed like a cowboy."

Her audience lets out a collective hmm.

"I was dining with a client, and Hermes entered the restaurant. I recognized him instantly despite his disguise and ordered him a drink. He joined our table and sat with my client and me."

"I saw your website," Noah says. "You sell your eggs?"

"Yes," Pam says and takes a bite of muffin.

"Your pictures, they show a lot," Noah adds.

"Clients want to know what I look like."

"What is this 'intimate experience' you offer for couples?"

Pam closes her eyes. "I like candy, flowers, romance, and dresses that show off my figure. I like to travel to exotic locations. I like being seduced and being the center of attention, sexually."

"It sounds like you should be paying them," Sharron grumbles.

"How does that work with a couple?" someone in the back asks.

Pam studies Sharron's expression while she describes the scene, enjoying the other woman's look of discomfort. "One person takes my top half, and the other gets the bottom. They switch as often as necessary until everyone's

210

needs are satisfied." After a bite of muffin and a sip of coffee, she asks. "Any more questions."

The room is quiet.

"No more questions, forever. Now go!"

The crowd scatters, leaving Maggie and Pam alone.

Pam takes a deep breath, holds it for ten beats, and then lets it out. "Feels so good to get that over and done with."

"Oh, that's never going to be over and done with, but it was worth it for Sharron's reaction, right?" Maggie grins. "You ready to bug out?"

"Definitely." Pam puts a hand on her belly. "In fact, this visit is a sort of goodbye. Colonel Baker says with the rice harvest over, my Interceptor is too valuable a target to sit in the harbor. So, I won't see you for a while."

"Wow. This is getting real."

211

Kim strides toward them, backpack swinging from her hand. "You ready?"

Pam stands. "Yup. I gave the townsfolk something to talk about for weeks."

Maggie hugs the two women before they leave.

They hall ass into Pam's electric pickup and drive south, past Hermes' house and through the back gate where two soldiers emerge from a concrete igloo. Antennas bristle across the domed roof like an outgrown buzzcut. They exchange greetings. Pam senses the guards' nervous excitement and can only imagine its effect on a telepath like Kim. A few miles further, they take a narrow road on the right that leads to the Bayou. Grass gives way to shrubs. As they get closer to the water, it's almost like they're driving through a tunnel. Massive trees stretch out their branches overhead like shaking hands with their neighbors. Pam flicks on the headlights to counter the gloom.

After a few miles, the oak trees reach Ceres' Harbor, where the Interceptor is anchored. Dave runs out of his boathouse and flags them down.

"Any news?" Pam asks.

"The blue elves are fighting with the green."

"What is it about this time?"

"Don't expect a dwarf to follow the arcana of elf logic."

Pam smiles, relieved that it's nothing serious. The two elf clans have fought over wild rice harvesting for decades. Pam parks the truck, and the two women board their houseboat. Dave throws them the rope, wishes them safe travels, and waves. Pam waves back and heads out of the harbor, the

Interceptor in tow. A crane watches them leave. On the main channel, they are surrounded by life. The chatter of birds is louder than the engine.

Kim puts a hand on Pam's shoulder. "So, how many GPS coordinates did you memorize?"

Colonel Baker has identified several hundred locations where houseboats can be hidden under a tree canopy. Pam has memorized them all.

"About three hundred and fifty."

"No backup on your phone?"

"Nope." Pam blushes.

"You're embarrassed."

A sacrodile makes a big splash with his tail. Pam steers the boat around him.

"It's my genetic engineering. I don't have a natural ability for eidetic imagery. I feel a little uncomfortable taking credit for someone else's work."

214

A yellow dashboard light turns on, indicating a microwave signal. Kim grabs a disposable drone and arms the EMP device. It's designed to fry electronics. She climbs the ladder to the crow's nest and releases the drone. Pam finds a shady spot and drops anchor. The drone hovers, waiting for a command. Kim climbs out of the crow's nest, sits in the passenger seat, and grabs the joystick plugged into a USB port. The drone ascends vertically. Kim performs a series of maneuvers that allow the Interceptor's computer to compare signals from the drone with the onboard microwave receiver. The computer displays the direction and heading of the microwave's source.

On top of the crow's nest is a high-definition camera. The boat's computer calculates the location and spots a commercial fixed-wing drone.

Kim flies the 5-blade helicopter drone on an intercept course to the fixed-wing craft. She keeps her eye on the screen, and soon, a green light flashes.

"It's gone, pit bull," Kim says, meaning the onboard microwave detector has locked onto the drone's transmitter, and the drone no longer needs Kim's guidance. In a few minutes, the high-def camera captures a white flash. The fixed-wing drone spirals slowly to the ground. Pam starts the engine and races to the soon-to-be crash sight. They lose sight of it in the trees and slow down.

Kim launches a second drone and spots the airplane in the treetops. Kim hops out of the boat and climbs while Pam watches the live feed and ensures no one approaches. After a tense twenty minutes, Kim returns with a six-foot wingspan aircraft. As soon as she's back on board, Pam lands their drone and returns to open water.

In minutes, they are headed to the main base under a grove of genetically engineered cedar trees. Kim keeps an eye on the microwave detector.

Kim stands at the bow when the base is in sight, proudly holding the captured drone high. Three houseboats are lashed together end to end. Airboats are tied to one side. Vanya greets us, and Kim hands the drone to her.

Before long, two elf women arrive with lunch and insist that Pam sits to be served. She decides there are some aspects of pregnancy that she might grow to love.

* * *

The Interceptor and a half dozen airboats hide under a canopy of trees a few miles from where Kim and Pam spotted the woodchip road. Vanya is in the passenger seat, staring at the dashboard screen. Using radio wave repeaters, the buried sensors will alert them if anyone approaches. Encrypted chatter has been way up in Frisco for the last few days, and the Colonel thinks an attack will happen soon.

Kim is sleeping in the back. Pam has been dozing, on and off, for the last few hours. It's 1:15 am. Pam opens the door and lets the night air and its frenetic sounds into the cabin. A croc swims around the parked airboats while pilots sleep. A yellow light blinks on the dashboard.

Vanya takes a sharp breath. "Show time."

Kim and the airboat pilots wake and rush to their stations.

Vanya keeps her eyes on the screen. Maps show pressure sensors going in and out of alarm mode as ATVs pass over them.

"It's a half-mile-long caravan. You ready to ruin their night?" Vanya asks.

"Light them up," Pam says.

Bounding anti-personnel mines leap into the air when the caravan is in position. A small propelling charge launches each mine three feet, and then the main charge detonates, spraying fragmentation at roughly waist height. Pam hears the report of detonations in the distance. She starts the engine and moves toward the chaos. As they get closer, they hear the sounds of small weapons firing. Kim and Vanya unpack more drones.

Radio waves have a good range but carry limited information. Only microwaves have the bandwidth for a live video feed. Vanya puts on a full emersion helmet and controls the flock of helicopter drones.

The drones use low power and maintain a 100-yard distance from each other to limit the risk of detection. The lead drones relay video along the chain to the Interceptor. Pam arrives at the prearranged spot with partial cover and drops anchor.

The drones zip in the direction of gunfire. Within minutes, infrared and low light cameras display the battlefield. The landmines did their job well, spraying metal into mercenaries. Bodies and RTVs with shredded tires litter the road. The convoy has been cut in half. A-Team is fighting the front while B-Team takes the rear column, and C-Team guards the landing site. Video from the drones reveals the mercenaries dressed in spider silk armor and additional Kevlar shell armor for their torsos. They're wearing helmets. However, they did not expect combat, and their necks and hands were exposed. Many lay wounded. The Navy's offensive uses M14s with armor-piercing rounds. The shell armor can stop a 30-caliber bullet from cutting through spider silk. The teams are kitted out with cyber implants and enhanced vision. Many soldiers are well-trained, and some are on loan from Navy units. With Vanya feeding the location of the front column's scattered forces, A-Team makes short work of the enemy. However, the B-Team meets with more resistance.

"Vanya, move half of A-Team to B-Team's position," Pam says. She takes a deep breath before issuing her next command. "Order the remaining A-Team to put a bullet through the heads of all wounded combatants, no exceptions. Then gather their communications equipment, weapons, etcetera and bring it all to the designated location."

Pam doesn't have a field commission, but Colonel Baker put her in charge of this operation, and he was very clear about how to take care of business.

"Take everything, including jewelry, anything that can be used for barter. Those are Colonel Baker's orders," she says over the airwaves to the A-Team leader.

"Roger that, out," Petty Officer Hernandez replies.

A yellow light blinks on the dashboard.

"Radio silence," Vanya says over the airwaves.

Vanya puts the drones in high-power mode. Now, 15 drones are pumping out microwaves while we maintain radio silence. High explosives crack a few hundred yards from our boat. We breathe a sigh of relief. The gunfire becomes sporadic and then stops. All but two drones return. Kim packs them away.

Vanya turns on one of the tablets Hermes made on his 3D printer. It's a text messenger that uses radio waves instead of microwaves. Fortunately, it's hard to detect.

"Vanya, text the pilots and tell them to prepare to take on cargo. Then, tell the people on standby to strip their boats and get over here."

Vanya types Pam's instructions on the tablet.

"The last convoy retreated into the forest," Vanya says.

223

Although Pam outranks her, Vanya knows combat. The latter mostly listens and learns from the more experienced officer. Minutes later, the airboats start to arrive. Pam uses binoculars to watch them load M16s onto the airboats.

Vanya receives another text. "Most of the equipment is in good shape. Half the ATVs are drivable, and they're well-equipped."

"I don't want to put the Navy Seals in harm's way, but we need to know whether there are weapons caches along the road."

"I'll ask some locals with sharp eyes to check it out," Vanya replies.

"Make sure they're well-armed."

Over the next hour, dozens of airboats are loaded and leave the bay. In the distance, they hear explosions.

"That's 120mm motor rounds," Vanya says.

Pam checks the time: 2:30 am. "The siege begins."

Towards dawn, more people arrive. Pam starts the Interceptor and maneuvers through the shallows, stopping near a group of people loading an airboat. She climbs into the crow's nest, and the fifty or so people look up at her.

"How many people want their own M16?" Pam asks.

Every hand is raised, including those belonging to the Navy Seals.

"If you take one, it means you are part of the militia and under the command of Colonel Baker. How many of you still want that M16?"

Everyone raises their hand, including Kim.

Kim smiles. "You can't have too many guns."

Pam scans the faces of the blue and green elf clans. "Who are your leaders?"

The elves look at each other.

"Okay, who's the best at organizing?"

Both the blue and the green elves look at a pot-bellied blue elf.

The de facto leader looks at Pam with narrow eyes and crossed arms. "What do I have to do?"

Pam gets out of her boat and approaches. "How many people do you trust that can shoot a rifle?"

He looks over the group. "Minus the people here, about thirty."

"Take one M16 each and 30 extras. Give the leader of each squad a tablet computer and let them know they're under the command of Colonel Baker."

He nods. "Okay, I can do that."

"Good. Now that's settled. We have until dawn to load supplies and leave."

Chapter Fifteen

The reverend breathes in the night air while his followers chant his name.

"Jim, Jim, Jim!"

He opens the app on his phone that controls his followers' emotions and selects a new feeling he hasn't used before—ecstatic joy—then presses send. He waits a few seconds and steps into the light.

The crowd shouts adulations. Jim allows them five minutes of pure joy at his sight before raising his hands. The followers quiet down and wait for their beloved leader to speak.

"God has spoken to me," he says, pausing for dramatic effect. "And what He has planned for you is wonderous. God's love and mercy are boundless. He is fair and justified in everything, never expecting more from us than we can give. The reverend pauses again. It's so quiet he can hear the leaves rustle.

"God sees your hard work to restore Frisco and wants to reward you with your own home." Again, he pauses.

"The town of Ceres will be your new home. You will never have to sleep on the streets again. You will never be hungry; you will never be cold. You can grow your own food on your own land."

People weep with joy.

"Ceres is the promised land. It's your home. Soon, very soon, you're going home."

Chapter Sixteen

Alone again, Colonel Baker's eyes track the dozen faces across the large screen in his conference room. They're all prepared for what he's about to say, but it doesn't make it any easier. This town has become his home. These people are his friends. Some of them may die soon.

"Our sources in Frisco say that a caravan of bikes and mini cars are assembling."

"How long before they reach us?" Sargent Conrad asks.

"A few hours at most," the colonel says. 'It's currently zero-one hours and fifteen minutes. I want everyone at their stations by zero-one-forty-five. Have your bug-out bags with you. We're not returning home."

The screens turn black individually as each leaves the conference to prepare. Everyone thinks they'll retake Ceres within a few months. James Baker knows that's not going to happen. The townspeople don't understand how dangerous a town like Ceres is to corporate power.

After the bio-wars, governments, having no money to pay their veterans, allowed them to trade pensions for land grants. As an army reserve base, Ceres is exempt from state, county and city taxes. Each home has its own well, septic and PV system, so there are no utility bills. The only costs are the upkeep of property and infrastructure.

Low-cost hemp construction destroyed the demand for stick-built homes. As a result, many states passed strict building codes to protect their corporate buddies. However, Ceres is exempt from state laws and building codes. In Ceres, with ten thousand credits in building materials and a little help from your friends, you can build a home over a weekend. You can move in once you put in a well and septic tank for five thousand credits. Then, people can take time to make improvements.

Ceres farms its own meat and vegetables while exporting enough rice to feed Frisco. The town's self-sufficiency is a threat to the corporations' all-pervading control.

Colonel Baker stands up and takes a final look around the conference room. Ten pounds of C4 sits on the table. He pushes a button, and the 'armed' light turns green. He salutes the empty room and then gently closes the door behind him. It will be years before he can return. It will be a war of attrition. The Ceres militia will conduct raids for minimal resources, forcing Baron to hire expensive guards to keep them out. Still, it will take years for Baron to realize he's made a costly mistake. When he finally asks to negotiate, the colonel or Hermes will kill Baron. James Baker hopes he will have that honor.

Outside, he gazes at the Bayou. The moon casts a silver glow across the water, making it look otherworldly. The colonel's ride is parked by the gate, an amphibious Light Armored Vehicle (LAV) with a crew of three: vehicle commander, gunner, and driver. Empty, it could hold an additional four passengers with combat gear, but the colonel's is fitted out with two computer stations and wall-mounted monitors.

Wearing a headset, Sergeant Rents sits at his station. Once the colonel is seated, the driver exits the gate. In less than a mile, they leave the road and drive under a thick canopy of genetically engineered cherry trees. Twenty minutes later, they are parked in the shade of mature trees north of the town center.

The gunner gets out and plugs into a port fitted into a metal fence post. A conduit from a nearby house provides them with a fiber optic line and coaxial cable. To hide their position, neither radio nor microwave broadcast is permitted.

The screens come alive. A drone near Frisco's north gate reveals the glow of electric bikes' headlights.

"How many?" Baker asks.

234

"The computer estimates a few thousand," Sargent Rents replies.

"They're cannon fodder to keep us busy. Baron wants to deplete our resources and ensure we are exhausted when the real fighting starts."

Twenty minutes later, the bikers arrive at Ceres' front gate. A barrage of 120mm mortars detonate sixty feet above their heads, producing a hailstorm of metal fragments. Body parts and broken bikes litter the pavement. Others ride around the carnage, and the motor fire adjusts. Finally, when the ground is too littered with debris to ride, people get off their bikes and run towards the front gate. Some make it past the death rain only to be taken out by snipers with M14s.

Another wave follows and meets the same fate. Finally, the eastern skyline brightens. The colonel checks his watch at 06:30.

"What's our inventory?"

"We're out of 120-millimeter motors. We still have half of the 82s and three-quarters of the 60s."

"How many dead?"

"The computer says a little over three thousand."

"That's the warm-up act. The main event will start around noon."

"When's the grand finale?" Sargent Rents asks.

"That depends on how long our mortars last."

Chapter Seventeen

The morning sun brings hope to many tired faces. Stevens commands a mortar brigade, mostly retired Navy from the Broadmoor subdivision. The team is unhappy about their Broadmoor homes being burned down and furious that Baron now threatens their new homes, houses they paid for in cash. They're so pissed. Many enjoy taking out their frustration on the bad guys with fragmentary mortars.

Stevens sees very little action from his position under the cherry trees. The mortars have been positioned so projectiles land in preselected targets. Spotters relay coordinates and Jessie gives the firing solution to the correct motor team. In another half hour, the first wave has been reduced to hunks of flesh, their blood soaking into the ground.

A woman with black hair and grey roots marches over. "Lt. Stevens, the 120mm team is moving to the first fallback location."

"Okay, how are we doing on ammo?"

"We have plenty of 60mm and a fair amount of 82s. But if we have another wave like that, we'll use up the 82s," Camila says.

"At least that means we won't have to lug them around."

Camila smiles. "Why don't we put the barrel and base plate on wheels and move them around rather than having all these metal tubes that may never be used littering the countryside?"

"Because a base plate and tube cost ten credits. Setting them up in advance is cheap, and we don't have to worry about sighting them during battle."

She shrugs. "Seems like a waste."

"A lot of things are wasted during the war. Why don't you lay down and try to sleep?"

Camila nods. "I'll lie down, but I don't think I'll sleep."

Stevens takes his own advice and lies in the shade of a cherry tree. The wind rustling the leaves lulls him to sleep.

* * *

He wakes when a hand touches his shoulder, unnerved that he did not hear the approach.

"Lieutenant, the next wave is on its way."

Stevens drags himself to his feet and checks his tablet computer. From the menu, he selects drone. The screen displays a caravan of bikes with cars and buses in the rear.

Around him, everyone stares at their own tablets, watching the bikes amass a few miles from the main gate. In less than an hour, cars and buses have joined the motorbikes. Soon after, they move forward as one. Again, with the bikes in front.

"Tablets down! Ear protection on!" Steven yells in a commanding voice.

The team puts away their equipment and ready the 60mm rounds. Stevens' screen lights up.

"Zone one, two, three, continuous fire!"

The crew of late middle-aged men and women go into action.

Mortars shoot up between the trees and rain metal at the front gate. Two hundred yards to Stevens' right, the 82mm rounds take out the raiders flanking the entrance.

The terrain around Ceres is hilly and covered in grasses and shrubs. A truck or jeep can drive around the fence. Unfortunately, the metal rain takes out many, but not all, vehicles.

Flamethrowers burn the thorny raspberry bushes. In minutes, the chain link fence is exposed.

The wave of bikes peaks. Stevens shouts, firing orders to his team. Soon, all zones are firing. Jessie helps a mortar team load missiles into the pipe. Within twenty minutes, they've made a significant dent in their stockpile of rounds.

Stevens checks his tablet and notes the fire damage to their perimeter fence. He can see people with bolt cutters attacking numerous sections. Sniper fire eventually takes them out. But they are replaced immediately by another, who picks up the bolt cutters and resumes work. After half an hour, the 82mm rounds are spent, and that team joins their compatriots in the 60mm teams. Stevens calls firing positions. They are down to one-third of their original mortar stockpile. He checks the tablet, and the drone video feed shows another wave of human beings being torn to shreds at the front gate. Their blood pools on the ground, yet stragglers charge with no hesitation. He tries to dispel negative thoughts by loading mortars.

Another wave charges toward breaks in the fence. Less than ten percent of the stockpile remains. The tablet flashes red to indicate a perimeter breach. He orders a firing squad to guard the perimeter. A few minutes later, he receives the order: 'zone 4A'. Their current position is zone 4B. It's time to move out.

He sends a global text, *Zone 4A*, before hopping in the cargo bed of his pickup. The tailgate is a half-inch of metal plate. He takes up a position with his M16 rifle. Mortars explode a hundred yards away. Metal rain shreds the trees, revealing enemy hordes running toward them. One man is missing his foot, and others are mortally wounded, but they keep moving. It makes no sense until Stevens recalls Kim and Hermes' report from Frisco about the nanite-infested water and its behavior-altering effects. He stares at the wounded, dying in their filthy, ragged clothes, and wonders. Each face expresses joy, not pain.

Stevens points his rifle, and his Mark 6 implant places a red dot in his field of vision. He puts the first bullet through Stumpy's eye, and the enemy dies. He keeps shooting while the mortar teams exhaust the last of their rounds.

A woman with a suicide vest explodes 30 yards away. Stevens is outside the blast zone, but two of his team are not so lucky. He fires above the rescuers' heads while they drag the wounded back to the trucks.

Someone keeps handing him fresh clips, but Stevens doesn't look away from the enemy to check who it is. Without the mortar fire, there are too many. Their position is overwhelmed.

Without waiting for Stevens' order, someone puts his truck into drive. The hordes give chase, but blood loss combined with a few miles of heavy cardio takes a toll on the cannon fodder. Nevertheless, Stevens keeps firing until they turn onto the main road. Only then does he look at his ammo supplier.

Anna gives him a thumbs-up. "That's some nice shooting. You're wasting your talent flying jets."

Chapter Eighteen

It's amazing what you can learn online. Colonel James wanted surface-to-air missiles to neutralize combat and troop-carrying helicopters. Usually, the army has a stockpile of stinger missiles, but corporations refuse to sell them. Since I have a 3D printer, I was responsible for making them.

I called a company that makes model rockets and ordered the biggest motor I could get without FAA approval. Natasha forged the necessary certifications, and six months later, 35 thrust-vectoring rocket motors were delivered. They're 5 inches in diameter and six feet long, including the payload. First, I downloaded the 3D files for the steering fins. Then, I used a Raspberry computer and downloaded the guidance system software.

Stinger missiles have a range of 3 miles and weigh 33 pounds. My rocket carries the same payload but has half the range and weighs almost twice as much. Since the youngest member of my crew is 62, the rocket launch tube is mounted on the back of quarter-ton pickups.

Stinger missiles use high-end hardware and software to find their target. My rockets rely on spotting crews shining high-intensity infrared and ultraviolet lasers on the helicopters. Their effectiveness is less than a mile, so the teams will be up close and personal with helicopters. Trucks will be targeted with actual stinger missiles and a 30mm machine gun. The corporations refuse to sell high-tech to the military while making plenty for their private armies. That's why my crew is so old. One has liver cancer. An 82-year-old who just had cathartic surgery is a driver. Our long-term survivability is zero.

Krypto and I sit in the shade and watch Ceres' airport. It's the most likely spot where Apache attack helicopters and Black Hawk troop carriers will land.

I check my tablet computer and learn that our perimeter has been breached in Zones 1, 2 and 3. It won't be long now.

Krypto gets up and growls at the Coastal Mountains.

Jason Baron has six troop carriers and two attack helicopters parked at an Aviation Center to the east of Ceres, near the old town of Napa.

Nestled between the mountains, the airstrip was built by the Army Corps during the Bio Wars. Its remote location and wide-open space means anyone approaching will be seen.

Soon, the wup, wup of Apache helicopters reaches my ears. They're above the mountains. I spot more helicopters coming from the north. I get out my rocket-powered grenade and launcher. In minutes, the attack helicopters patrol while the troop carriers prepare for landing on an airstrip one mile long.

Natasha counts down. *"Three, two, one."*

From the eastern tree line, seven rockets are launched. Three hit their mark. Only 400 people have stayed to defend Ceres. There are 200 on mortar crews. One hundred guard the back gate and the harbor. Leaving 100 for rifle and rocket crews. Only 50 of those guard the airport.

One gunship's back rotor is torn to pieces; the helicopter spins to the ground sideways, and the rotor chucks fly. The other gunship's 30mm cannon gives a short burst of rounds that hit a cache of our rockets. A few whirl in circles, narrowly missing the helicopter. Others explode, enveloping the area with a white cloud of burning rocket fuel.

An RPG is accurate to 1,000 feet, but the action is over 1,600 feet away. Natasha calculates the arc, and I fire. The missile corkscrews and lands near a troop carrier. Pieces of asphalt fly up and damage the rear blade.

Adding to the epic cluster fuck, I arc another over, not bothering to look. Instead, I join Krypto on my electric bike. Hunched over, I twist the throttle and get out of there. I weave through trees at 60mph. Behind me, a hellfire missile destroys my cache of RPGs. There are stockpiles everywhere around Ceres. Many people who ride dirt bikes are part of the mobile grenadier squad.

I head to the next probable landing site, a goat pasture. Cutting through the trees, I'm there in minutes. I use a house as cover and find the weapons in a plastic trash can. On the other side of the house, a helicopter lands. I load the weapon and peek around the corner. A squad of men is coming my way. I aim for the lead mercenary and fire. I can't wait to see what happens.

I run to my bike, and Krypto is already aboard. The blast is followed by gunfire, but I'm nowhere near them.

"Hermes," Natasha says. *"Colonel Baker orders you to evacuate*

immediately. Navy intelligence decoded a message. A special team was sent to kill you."

I have an airboat stashed near my rice plantation. Another at Teshi's place by the water. But both locations are easy to ambush. Instead, I head due west to the Coastal Mountains.

The rice silos are on high ground to the west. They're empty. During the day, conveyer belts loaded the silos. Then, at night, trucks haul them out in 55-gallon barrels.

I find a break in the west chain-link fence, hidden behind a thick section of raspberry bushes. I put on heavy gloves, pull the spikey vines to the side and push my bike through. Krypto follows. After untangling my jacket from the thorns, I guide my bike into a ditch that leads to a tunnel that passes under the clear area surrounding the perimeter fence.

One hundred yards of near-complete darkness later, the culvert slopes upward and leads to a trapdoor. I push it open, walk my bike out of the tunnel and close it behind me. I use leaf litter to disguise the door and look around. The spruce trees are old-growth.

I like this section of the forest; the carpet of needles absorbs sound. The only noise comes from the trees as they creak in the wind, the sounds of battle too quiet to detect.

I find one of many dirt bike trails and head north, twenty miles to the rallying point. Instead of getting into the Zen of trail riding, I can't shake the feeling that I'm being followed. I push the button, and my bike switches to battery-saving mode.

Usually, I am careful with security and scan for trackers every few days. But with last week's last-minute preparations, I became lax. My gut tells me my bike has a GPS tracker. I don't want to lead the enemy to the rally point, so I meander, taking random trails until my spare battery runs out of power. I take a few minutes to spin off the wing nuts and remove the dead weight. I'm still carrying an RPG launcher strapped to my bike, plus the two grenades I'm sitting on. If they're coming for me, I won't make it easy.

I check my virtual watch at 4:38 pm. Sunset isn't until 6:08. I am halfway through a protein bar when I feel like walls are closing in on me. I give Krypto the rest of the bar and put on my riding gloves.

Krypto hops on, and we continue north for another dozen miles, where I stop and check my tablet's GPS. From here, the rally point is five miles east. I keep going north. The dirt bike trail narrows into a game path. Finally, after another three miles, I stop. There is a river a few hundred yards ahead; the Cache Creek Trail will take me directly to the rally point eight miles southeast.

The only thing I take from the bike is an empty 12-ounce water bottle. No one lives this far north, so Cache Creek water is pristine.

First, I unclip the rocket launcher from my bike and hide it in the brush. Then, I check my vest pockets and locate two small devices I made on my 3D printer. I fit them over the tip of the RPG grenade. Then, grab a spare pair of socks but leave the rest of the clothes; my feet will get wet on the trail. I carefully close the compartment after flipping the switch that arms the devices. A vibration sensor will send a signal to ignite a half-ounce of thermite, which will ignite the grenade fuse.

I march 200 yards to the trailhead and look around. Birds fill the trees that line the creek. I tuck my pants into my socks and jog at an eight-minute mile pace. It allows me to watch the trail and keep plenty in reserve for a sprint. Birds scold me as I pass.

The trail is in good shape for the first half hour, but the next section was washed out when the creek changed course. Feeling exposed, I cross the ankle-deep water as quickly as I can. On the other side, I hear an explosion while considering the merits of changing my socks.

Krypto looks at me and then takes the lead. I check my virtual watch—at 5:50 pm. Eighteen minutes to sunset. I think the squishing sounds of my water-filled shoes are deafening until a hellhound howls ahead. Behind me, the river carries the faint whine of an electric motor.

Krypto howls back. He's only six months old, and his howling needs work. The whine of motors is getting closer, so I pick up the pace. I realize I haven't had this much fun since Vegas. I wait for a headlight to find me. I don't have to wait long. A beam strikes my back, and I bolt into the forest. The M16 report makes me chuckle because I know what will happen next. Initially, I would sprinkle the new sphere LEDs on the ground and then toss a few EMP grenades about to fry their electronics; instead, I stand next to a tree and wait.

Once upon a time, the Titans gave me a crystal to put into the mainframe of a hellhound growing factory. A few of my skin cells clung to the crystal, enough to transfer the necessary genes to give hellhounds freewill. For some reason, it also changed combat and sex androids. To cut a long story short, combat androids refuse to fight, and sexbots have unionized. Oh, and I almost forgot the most relevant part: hellhounds love me.

The lead bike stops and turns into the forest. Three other cycles follow. In a few seconds, their headlights illuminate me again. They stop, point their weapons, and dismount. The lead man removes his damaged helmet and grins. Half his face is pocked, marked by recent shrapnel.

"You have given us a merry chase," he says, walking closer. "But it's the end of the road for you."

Cold creeps over my skin. Sunset. "Yes, it is the end of the road."

One assassin puts away their rifle, gets a cell phone, and records. I guess they need proof to be paid. Behind the killers, a huge branch snaps.

I act like the bad boy. "Do you know what that is? Huh?" That's an 800-pound hellhound using his prehensile claw to rip a large branch off a tree."

The four form a defensive circle.

I sing and dance. "Whatcha gonna do when they come for you?"

A hellhound lazily walks into the light.

"Do you see her self-confidence? I know those M16s with armor-piercing rounds will not penetrate hellhound armor. You need an armored troll with a 50-caliber machine gun for a fair fight." I saunter across and stand beside the beast, my head level with its shoulders.

"And since *I* know that, *she* knows that."

The hellhound grins, and they take a step back.

"You might want to put those weapons down; otherwise, she may think you are trying to hurt me."

They lower their weapons.

I give a well-practiced sardonic grin. "Those are nice vests, and those helmets look super high-techy. I'll trade you one of each for a five-minute head start."

In seconds, I get my well-deserved reward, and they turn their bikes around and leave the way they came. Krypto barks and growls as the assassins depart. I chuckle, knowing that a pack of hellhounds is in the area, and they're already positioned to pick the assassins off individually. I get my night vision goggles out of a vest pocket and put them on.

I look down at Krypto. "We got six more miles before dinner time."

His whole body wags. I thank the adult hellhound, and Krypto and I continue down the trail.

Chapter Nineteen

"Colonel, Zones one, two and three are breached."

The wall-mounted monitors reveal to the colonel the effects of those breaches. Hundreds of people pour through multiple openings.

"Fall back to zone five and tell the troops guarding the back gate to make final preparations."

"Roger that," Sargent Rents says.

The eight-wheeled amphibious armored reconnaissance vehicle moves forward. A caravan of light trucks follows behind. In five minutes, they reach the rally point. Trucks break formation, hide under the trees, and the mortar teams set up.

"Sir, we have helicopters inbound."

"Alert the grenadier teams."

The colonel's Light Armored Vehicle has a 25mm Gatling cannon and two missile pods, each capable of holding four stinger missiles. However, stocks are depleted. They're down to the last three. Despite Hermes' workarounds, the corporations' embargo on selling weapons to the army has been effective.

Colonel James Baker places his hand on Sergeant Rents' shoulder. "Turn on the radar."

A half dozen boat radar systems are tied into Ceres' sensor net. In seconds, the screen shows eight helicopters inbound.

"Light up the tattlers."

Tattlers are devices that Hermes invented. They're bluffs designed to make the enemy believe you are heavily armed. He printed out a few dozen of these devices. When they are lit up, the enemy should be fooled into thinking they are being targeted by laser-guided missiles. The colonel is not superstitious but crosses his fingers and prays the tactic works.

Sargent Rents chuckles when the helicopters take evasive maneuvers and drop flares. Soon, the helicopters target what they believe to be anti-aircraft weapons, and the enemy's rockets take them out, wasting a dozen missiles on laser pointers, exactly as the colonel intended.

The helicopters head to the airport. In minutes, 25mm cannons and rocket power grenades fly through the air.

An airport camera shows one of Hermes' homemade rockets hit an Apache attack helicopter. Then, a cache of missiles explodes, and the camera view is obscured by white smoke.

The mortar fire begins again. With the mass of people rushing to the town center, the exploding shells cartwheel body parts through the air. Corpses are sprawled across the main road, and ditches run red with blood.

Eight helicopters invaded Ceres' airspace, but only three remain. The enemy flanks them to the west, but rifle teams keep them at bay. Injured attackers limp onward for the next few hours and are taken out by snipers. They keep coming.

The mortar teams take a break; they have been awake since before dawn, and the day is catching up with them. Twenty minutes later, another wave of people hits the main gate.

"How many mortars?" the colonel asks.

Sargent Rents consults the computer, requesting it displays the percentage reserves for each firing team. "The average is eighty percent, sir."

The next wave arrives, and the mortars rain death.

"I don't get it," Sargent Rents says. "They could deploy countermeasures to suppress mortar fire, but they don't."

"Baron wants us to kill them. They have served their purpose by exhausting our reserves, and now they are literally and figurately cannon fodder."

"Can we reason with these people? Perhaps stop the carnage?"

"They have implants controlling their emotions. They can't be reasoned with."

"So, Baron turned these people into zombies and pointed them in our direction."

The colonel nods. "There's nothing we can do for them."

During the following fifty minutes, Colonel Baker watches their mortar reserves dwindle to less than ten percent, and knows another wave is all it will take to overrun their position.

"Fall back, everyone, to the back gate."

Mortar teams race to their trucks while the rifle teams hop in the back. Then, just like drilled, the town center is abandoned in minutes. What remains is a saddening sight. Most of the PV panels have been stripped from their frames. Maggie's Bakery is bordered shut. The town is abandoned, lost to oceans of the dead. Only ghosts remain. The colonel knew it was only a matter of time before Ceres and other small towns became too prosperous. Like mobsters, the corporations envied Ceres' wealth and wanted it for themselves. However, homes have been stripped to the bare bones over the last six months. The harvest was hidden, and people's possessions were stored at the Navy base. Baron will find only slim pickings here.

Due to their reliance on shipbuilders, the Navy has deep ties to corporations and must remain officially neutral. Unofficially, the base commander is sympathetic.

At 18:20 hours, they arrive at the back gate. It's been a long and arduous day, but their casualties are few. Everyone is leaving in electric pickups.

Some are heading to the Navy base. Others will join the remaining resistance in the Bayou. The Light Armored Vehicle port is plugged into sensors, and the screen lights up. Yet another mass of suicidal bikers swarms their way. These are riding dirt bikes, and the lead attackers will reach their position within minutes.

"Arm the minefield."

Sargent Rents types and red lights pox mark the map of Ceres. They hear a distant explosion and a red light blinks out. The lead bikes are removed by road mines, adding hazards to the enemy's journey. Nevertheless, the pack carefully picks its way through the maze, and the bikers are in sight before long. With M14 rifles, the 30-caliber rounds knock them off their bikes. Against the maddening horde, eighty Ceres soldiers defend the back gate and their exit into the forest. At first, it's one-sided—a slaughter that will provoke nightmares for years. Then, a suicide vest explodes, and another goes off, creating a hole in Ceres' defenses. A gunner fires the 25mm cannon, then a rocket-powered grenade goes off near the LAV.

"Sargent Rents, order the retreat."

"Damn, I thought we would win for a moment."

"Their main act, Sargent, is already through the front gate. No more cannon fodder. These are well-equipped mercenaries."

"Roger that," Rents says and sends the order.

Smoke encompasses the fence line and the one-hundred-yard buffer beyond. Two automatic sentry machine guns cover their exit. Soldiers quickly slip into the forest. The colonel's LAV is the last to leave. Charges are detonated at the back gate once they have crossed the cleared zone. The ground rumbles from multiple detonations. The shaking sets off Hermes' booby trap. A green fireball rises high over his house. A sharp hiss in the colonel's helmet mic tells him Hermes added an EMP kick. The kid always puts on one hell of a show.

Chapter Twenty

It's been a year since the fall of Ceres, and the remaining resistance fighters celebrate Halloween under a canopy of oaks amongst mangrove roots. An apple cider pressing contest turns into a pulp-throwing free-for-all all. There is no clear winner. Everyone is equally covered in the stuff. The laughter is music to everyone's ears— healing.

Hermes tells spooky stories to the kids by the campfire. He does his fogging-the-area trick, and the children squeal delightfully.

Brigette, Pam and Hermes' daughter, sleeps on Pam's lap. She's seven months old and DARPA-baby strong. Many of Colonel Baker's soldiers were in the DARPA super-soldier program, and one in three children inherited their parents' superior strength and endurance. In Hermes, those genes are latent but fully expressed in his daughter.

Jessie sits beside Pam, who leans against a rock. "Hermes is taking Brigette for a few days so I can get some quality time with my husband."

Jessie wraps his arm around her. "Life doesn't get better than this."

"I wouldn't say no to a hot shower."

"I don't think it will be too much longer. While Baron publicly gloats about his victory, the colonel plots his demise."

273

"And us pawns get moved around the chessboard," Pam says.

"Na, you're the bishop or rook, at least with your Interceptor."

"So, who's the queen?" Pam asks.

Hermes throws powder into the fire, making green flames leap into the air. Children scream.

"Oh yeah," Pam says. "There's our queen bee."

Part Three

Restoration

Chapter Twenty-One

We're sitting around a cold campfire pit. We cannot risk exposing our location by lighting a fire with all of us meeting. It's been four-and-a-half years since the fall of Ceres.

I miss my garden and home. I'm not good on the water, and neither is Krypto. We need trees, shade, and room to work our magic. Krypto's fur is so black he blends with the night. Only his red eyes and gleaming claws betray his presence.

He is pretending to sleep next to me, but from how his ears constantly move and his nostrils twitch, I can tell he's anxious. His fear is contagious. My flesh tingles with it.

Lieutenant Garry Rents arrives. He received a field commission two years ago, and his new rank reflects this promotion. We start the meeting.

"Is everyone on board with the plan?" Colonel James asks.

Ceres, technically, remains a U.S. Army reserve base, although we have been kicked off our land. Hundreds of reserve bases and Army towns pepper the states. Since the fall of Ceres, more are coming under pressure.

"I still don't like it," I say. "I feel like we're stooping to their level."

"We are," my father, Daniel, says. "During the depression, the bank robbers had better guns and cars than local police. So, law enforcement adopted their tactics and used them against them. Think of us like them if it helps."

I shrug my shoulders. "Natasha has already made up her mind, so the decision is out of my hands."

"Do you think it will work?" Lieutenant Rents asks.

I nod. "So far, our raids have annoyed them. Baron has beefed up security. However, we've lulled the town into a false sense of security. Baron believes he's won. That's why we haven't breached the perimeter for nine months. They've started holding events at the new Ceres County Club. Pride comes before a fall. The town is ripe for attack."

"Hermes is spot on, and we've never attacked during the day," Daniel says. "They think they're safe. Civilian deaths will hurt Baron's corporate image. If he doesn't retaliate, he'll look weak."

"I have to agree. Baron's a man who holds a grudge," I say.

Colonel James nods. "He doesn't know our resources. There are several thousand residents of the Sacramento Bayou. All of them are very concerned about what happened to Ceres. Hopefully, Baron will act rashly, and we can capitalize on his mistake."

"My brigade is ready," Lieutenant Rents says. "They're itching for a fight."

"I'll need a few more weeks with the new recruits," Daniel says.

Pam checks her satellite phone. "Ceres' Country Club is having a wedding. One of Baron's business partners, Charles Whitmore, booked the venue. His son is getting married."

Colonel James' finger traces the scar on his cheek. "That's three weeks from now. After our attack, Baron's ego will be bruised, so we can expect a swift counterattack."

"We'll be ready," Daniel says.

"How about you, Hermes? You ready?" Colonel James asks.

"I will be. And sure, I get it. Baron's security is too dug in for us to retake Ceres by conventional methods. We have to fight dirty. I don't like the terrorist approach. However, I dislike even more not being able to sleep in my bed."

"Then we are in agreement," Colonel Baker says, looking at each of us. We all nod in acknowledgment of our pact.

Chapter Twenty-Two

I stand topside on my semi-submersible houseboat, where I tend my primitive garden, a sandbar with native grasses and shrubs, and the cherry tree Kukan gave me. It's taller than me now and needs a bigger pot.

"I know you want real soil and a permanent home. So do I."

"Who are you talking to?" Daniel notices the tree and smiles. "You and your mom have green thumbs."

"I miss gardening."

Daniel changes the subject. "They're ready for you."

I force a smile and follow my father down the hatch and close it behind us. The ladder descends into the utility room with a washer, dryer and hot water heater. They are all electric and powered by a thorium reactor. We cross through the kitchen and into a living room lined with monitors. People sit at each station except the one left for me.

Going old school, I plug a fiber optic cable into the back of my ear and the other end into a USB port on the computer. Natasha connects with our fleet of drones. It's a mixture of five-blade helicopters, surveillance crows and suicide doves. I chose to pack high explosives into dove drones because male doves kill their rivals. After years in the field, I'm developing a taste for irony.

A five-mile fiber-optic cable was recently laid through the rice fields to ensure we're not detected. On the other end is an airboat with a transmitter. My autonomous blackbird drones are already in place. The three birds have eyes on Ceres Country Club while four others act as relays so the signal reaches us.

Our helicopter drones are inbound. The graphene capacitor batteries give them extra range. I check the feed and quickly count attendance— about 200 people celebrate the wedding.

"I have control of the drones," Natasha says.

My heart skips a beat. A feeling of dread descends on me. These are civilians, not soldiers. I know my plan will work. We are about to murder 200 people, a few of whom are legitimate targets. I brush a tear from my cheek and swallow my regret.

Surveillance crows map the helicopters' route, easily escaping detection. At 60 miles an hour, the drones close the distance to the country club.

Baron's construction teams demolished our school and installed a golf course. It's a lovely building.

The helicopter drones are seconds away. Suicide doves, packed with pound C4 and screws, fly over the audience. They detonate simultaneously. A few seconds later, helicopter drones with a few ounces of C4 dive into the wedding party. The bride, groom, every wedding official, three bridesmaids, and the best man are targeted with precision. A drone hovers at eye level in front of each face.

"Now!" Colonel James orders.

I close my eyes as Natasha presses the trigger.

A mist of flesh and blood obscures the crows' vision. When it clears, bodies lay scattered on the ground; their heads and necks are missing.

The remaining drones descend on anything still moving. Within seconds, the attack is over. A blackbird drone flies in a circle and then perches on the roof. We bear witness as Security rushes to the scene and looks for survivors. One man slips into the lake of blood and falls.

Crow drones record the aftermath for a few minutes before heading home.

Daniel puts his hand on my shoulder. "You would have been an excellent field commander."

I swallow bile and glare at his manicured fingernails. "I am an

285

excellent field commander. I didn't have to join the army to figure that out."

Daniel nods. "That you are. And all you had to do is listen to Colonel Baker instead of arguing with him."

"I'm cooperating because I want my life back."

"So do I, son; we all do. And we appreciate what you and Natasha bring to the table."

I look at my feet. "We just murdered 200 people. Doesn't that bother you? Do you have a conscience?"

"Not really. DARPA babies don't experience fear or remorse. Sometimes, we fake it."

It's a moment of honesty that explains so much of my childhood.

Chapter Twenty-Three

We're sitting around the cold campfire pit. Krypto is to my right, and my father is to my left. Colonel James sits across from me. His complexion is a tad more yellow than usual.

"Well, that worked," Garry Rents says. "They're assembling a strike team as we speak."

"How many?" I ask.

"Rumor mill says 200 mercenaries. They have three Interceptors in Ceres' harbor with anti-drone missile systems."

"We can mine the choke points in the channels," Pam says. "I have a team with a 3D printer. All we need is C4."

Colonel James nods. "Make a list, and Lieutenant Rents will see you get what you need."

Garry nods.

"Navy Intel says Baron hired an additional twenty mercs with powered armor. We need to neutralize that threat," the colonel says.

"All that hardware needs software to run. An EMP bomb should take them out." I reply.

"The suits are hardened to microwaves," Garry says.

"To a particular threshold. If we exceed that, the electronics are toast. But it's risky. A big enough bomb will be hard to transport. What we need is an edge. Something I can steal without anyone realizing until we use it." I smile. "Does Navy Intel have a wish list?"

"I'll check into it," Colonel James says. "Anything else."

"One last thing. Is there a reason why Krypto's shit glows in the dark?" Garry asks.

I pull a marble-sized LED sphere from my vest pocket. I turn it on, and it glows green. Krypto looks at me and wags his tail. I toss the sphere, and he leaps, catching it mid-flight and snapping his jaws shut around the glowing ball.

"I see," Garry says. "So, why does he eat them?"

"I think he likes seeing his poo in the dark, make sure it doesn't go anywhere."

"Wow, that's taking anal retentive to a new level."

Everyone laughs. Krypto mimics our reactions by exposing his teeth and making he-he-he sounds.

"Maybe you should have named him Mutley," Garry quips.

The laughter feels good, healing.

Chapter Twenty-Four

Weapon manufacturers refuse to sell heavy weapons to the federal government and supply them solely to their corporate friends. They aim to replace elected governments with corporate governance to repeal the Bill of Rights.

So, it turns out the U.S. Navy and Army have long wish lists. There is a weapons depot near Death Valley. The closest landmark is the old town of Bishop, California. The only remaining resident is an older man in a mobile home. I set him up in a four-star hotel in Los Angeles with a 500 credit-a-day allowance.

I sit in his lawn chair with a pair of binoculars. The twenty-acre weapons facility is fully automated. Only three employees work the midnight shift. One guards the gatehouse. Two others sit in front of monitors.

The swing shift workers leave right on time at one am. I rap on the trailer door. Kim and Stevens are inside with the air conditioner on full. I've become accustomed to the 95-degree temperatures after sundown.

We wear ultra-black clothes and baseball caps. Masks hang around our necks. Stevens and I adjust our goggles to low light, and Kim takes the lead. Her peripheral vision is vastly superior to ours.

It's a two-mile march to the chain link fence. We keep away from the red glow of LEDs mounted on posts. We pause 100 yards away from the east wall. There isn't a door or window in sight for 350 yards. We trek north toward the heat pumps, where there's an entrance to the warehouse.

We pull up our face masks and pull our caps down. I hold out my hands; Stevens takes my left and Kim my right. We take a few steps forward, and a web of shadows crisscrosses my hands, chilling my flesh. I stare at the northeast corner of the building and let the shadows take me in. Kim and Stevens have been practicing and have no fear when the darkness swallows us. For an instant, we cease to exist. I recall the corner, and we're standing right next to it.

While Kim and Jessie recover, I peek around the corner. The door has an electronic keypad and a wireless interface. Natasha unlocks it and spoofs the camera above the door. It senses a voltage spike and shuts down for three seconds. Stevens opens the door, and we move quickly through.

"How long, Natasha," I whisper.

"Two point eight seconds."

I smile. "Easy peasy, lemon squeezy."

The automated warehouse is filled with microwave repeaters. Natasha uses one to find the nearest terminal from which she can control the computerized forklifts. Since forklifts move about constantly, we avoid cameras, and there are no motion sensors.

I take the lead, and Natasha guides us to the closest terminal. It turns on.

Stevens looks over my shoulder. "Natasha, you are so good at hacking into systems, quite possibly the best."

Natasha pulls up a list and highlights any torpedoes with above state-of-the-art electronics. *"They come in a pack of two if that's okay,"* Natasha purrs.

I roll my eyes. I can't believe even Natasha falls for Jessie's charm. While Natasha locates items from everyone's wish lists, I search for something special, just for me.

"Ah," says Kim, looking over my other shoulder.

"Who wants a hoverbike? It has a state-of-the-art graphene supercapacitor battery with twice the energy density of gasoline. They're still in boxes, so we must put them together."

I wouldn't say no to a hoverbike," Stevens says.

"What do they look like?" Kim asks.

"Why? Do you want a pink one with unicorns?"

She punches my shoulder. I probably deserve it.

"They're similar to the five-blade helicopters with a seat mounted in the center and three-hundred pounds carrying capacity."

"Yeah, I'll take one," Kim says.

Natasha sends forklifts to retrieve the items, including six hoverbikes. We still have a little room to spare.

"Natasha, what do you want."

"A Learjet, but they don't have one here."

"Okay, what's your number two pick that's not a plane?"

"There's an anti-drone and missile defense system with a megawatt laser. If we return two hoverbikes, it'll fit in the trailer."

"The sacrifices I have to make...
Okay, but only because it's you."

"Thank you, darling."

A semi-truck and attached trailer reverses into the loading dock. The robot forklifts load the cargo. The entire operation takes less than an hour. As the truck pulls away from the pier, Natasha alerts the spotter team and erases our order from the database, so it looks like the vehicle was empty when it left.

We exit through the same door as we entered, shift to the fence, and head back to the east wall. Kim takes the lead again as we return to our rented home. We pack up in under two minutes and get in a beat-up VW bus. It was serviced the day before we left and cranks on the first try. In minutes, we're heading north on the highway.

Kim sits in the passage seat with her foot on the dash. I drive.

"That's it," Natasha says half-an-hour later. *"The truck has been successfully intercepted. The cargo is in our possession."*

Now that the job is over, we all sigh in relief.

Chapter Twenty-Five

The base is a series of huts that constitute the blue elves' winter home. Around 200 elves live here. Unlike the hemp houses of Ceres these are made of living vines twined around bamboo scaffolding. The stream that flows lazily through the village is adequate for all their water needs.

There are two clans of elves in the Bayou: green and blue. Their pigmented skins efficiently convert light into sugar. Most have webbed toes, and one in six have lungs and gills. Both clans harvest wild rice as a cash crop to trade or sell.

Sargent Crandell walks in and salutes. "They're ready for you."

Lieutenant Rents exits his hut, and the soldiers stand to attention. He surveys the 80 men and women who have volunteered for this high-risk mission. "At ease."

The soldiers stand at parade rest. They're a mixture of green and blue elves and Ceres' residents. None wear army uniforms.

"Our mission is simple: put up a hell of a fight so the enemy sees only us and not the trap they're walking into. Once the trap is set, we haul ass into the tunnels and put as much distance between us and the decades-old dynamite and C4 as possible."

Everyone nods.

"If any powered armor suits come your way, run. Those babies stop anything short of 50-caliber rounds, so leave the mercs in metal suits alone; that's an order. Another team will deal with them. Corporations claim our rights interfere with their profits. We all know what is at stake. They took our land, and we want it back." Rents make a fist. "We will crush them. When we are done with the corporate mercs, their assholes will pucker shut whenever they hear the words Sacramento Bayou."

The soldiers cheer.

"Navy intel says boats are inbound; it won't be long now, so take your last piss and get to your stations. Dismissed."

The entrances to the system of tunnels are hidden inside huts. A thousand-watt generator powers the surveillance cameras and intercom system. Rents are the last to enter.

Ten minutes later, the east and south perimeter guards fire on the armored chest plates and helmets of the approaching mercenaries. The enemy returns fire with M16s. Rocket-propelled grenades pound the fortifications. The west perimeter guards are firing on intruders, and soon, the team to the north is engaged in battle. Rents signal it's time to fall back.

"We're surrounded," Rents reports on the intercom.

Machine gun emplacements grow silent as the enemy moves closer to the inner defenses.

With everyone underground, Rents shouts over the RPGs, "All wounded to evac now. Get the fuck out of here!" Dirt falls from the ceiling. An explosive charge opens the entrance to the underground fortress.

While the wounded evacuate, the remaining defenders display nerves of steel as the enemy enters the tunnels.

They hold out for another 14 minutes and then Rents shouts his last order. "Time to bug out, now!"

Soldiers rush past him and down the tunnel. It is time for the sound and light show. Rents switches on the speakers and blasts the sounds of firing M16s. Lights strobe to mimic muzzle flash. Bullets pepper the wall to his right. He sprints for 200 yards until he reaches an exit that surfaces under a canopy of oaks. He sets a charge near the mouth of the tunnel. The small explosion causes the roof to collapse and sends a shock wave that starts a timer. Rents hide in the ditch they cut a few days earlier. When the blast hits, Rents and his team are lifted a few inches in the air. The crack of the shock wave activates the noise suppression in Rents' helmet. Dirt and pieces of wood rain down on them.

After the sounds of battle, the silence seems deafening. Then, like zombies, his squad rises from the earth.

Chapter Twenty-Six

Many lessons were learned while defending Ceres. The rocket-powered grenade teams on electric bikes were highly effective, but the teams in pickups were sitting ducks.

This time, my mobile brigade consists of ten trolls in body armor riding ATVs and another ten teenagers on electric bikes armed with RPGs. Natasha guides the crow drones and a new condor drone that rides the thermals along the Coastal Mountains.

Yesterday, Navy intelligence warned us that Baron has readied six helicopters. Two are Apache attackcopters, and the remaining four are designed to transport mercenaries in heavy armor and weapons. Their powered suits have a relatively short battery life, so they'll want to land within a mile of our position to conserve energy for the fight.

"Darling, the helicopters are in the air."

"Roger that," I say.

Natasha alerts my team, and the trolls start their engines.

The condor channel shows the Apache helicopters in front, deploying flares. The four troop carriers follow, with the condor trailing them. The drone feeds Natasha the GPS coordinates, and we know where they are headed. A burn area from a lightning strike downed a half dozen trees. It's a mile away. The trolls take the lead with the grenadiers on electric bikes behind them. I'm last and carrying our secret weapon. I got the idea from a show on the Autonomous Snake Channel where people compete to make the most realistic snake. I downloaded the 3D STL files and printed my own with a twist. Next to the spinal column is a detonating cord used to cut steel. I set it to target the weakest points, where body armor is designed to flex, like an ankle.

I hear M16s behind us. The siege has begun. We press forward and stop where oak trees block direct sunlight, allowing only patches of dappled light to break through the canopy. Blackbird and crow drones take their positions, providing a secure radio and microwave network.

Within minutes, we hear sounds of brush crunching under armored boots. The noise is coming closer. The trolls take up position and fire short bursts from 50-caliber machine guns at the mercenaries. They return fire with 308s, rounds ping off the trolls' armor.

I open my bag and release the snakes. Navy intelligence says twenty armored bad guys, but to be sure, I made a hundred snakes. I free the first fifty, and Natasha uses bird drones to guide them.

The attackers change to 50-caliber weapons. Grenadiers step out from behind the trolls and fire RPGs. The mercenaries are 50 yards away, so there are only five direct hits. The others drop to the ground and keep firing. Six of my ten grenadiers take a hit, and the 50-caliber rounds rip limbs from their bodies.

I release the remaining snakes while the trolls fall back. My crew all wear transmitters that emit a frequency to repel the mechanical snakes.

The remaining fifteen mercenaries lay down a wall of fire that fells trees. I drop to the ground and crawl. Soon, the men redirect their weapons and fire at the ground. One armored mercenary drops, then another. They are targeting the snakes but are overwhelmed by numbers. When they eventually decide there are too many snakes and run, the surviving grenadiers pick them off. I signal to the trolls to cease fire, and the din of battle drops. Between the short bursts of enemy fire, I can hear their screams. Every ten seconds, a loud pop as 18 inches of detonation cord explodes.

I walk closer, and my team follows.

"No! No! NO!" someone screams, then a pop.

A young man in his early twenties is trying to bury his feet and hands in his lap. He looks up at me with tears running down his face. "I want my mommy!"

I watch with morbid fascination as a snake climbs his spine and disappears down his neckline. Finally, he stops crying. His eyes plead with me to stop it. A muffled pop from under his armor sends a shock wave through his body. His eyes go dull, and then he slumps forward.

I survey the carnage. The snakes, dutiful to their programming, chop up the mercs at their joints. Yet, for all the dismemberment, there's little blood. The heat from the high explosive charge cauterizes the wounds. We unfasten the armor and load it on the ATVs.

A young man with a scraggly five-o'clock shadow looks at me. With his missing limbs, the merc is literally and figuratively a basket case. "Aren't you gonna kill me?"

"Why? It's a waste of good ammo, and what's in it for me?"

"Are you Conrad?"

"Yeah, I'm a Conrad."

"They told us you were only dangerous at night."

"No, but I'm less dangerous during the day."

"I'll include that in the debriefing, assuming someone comes for me."

"Before the coyotes arrive," I say.

Chapter Twenty-Seven

Six field officers convene at the unlit campfire pit. Major Hayes has joined them for the first time in a year. For security reasons, she and Colonel Baker are rarely together.

"It worked. Baron wants to negotiate," Colonel Baker says.

"Do you think it's a trap?" Hermes asks.

"That's not the way Baron works. He'll arrange a meeting and have his lawyers come in his stead. They'll threaten me with legal action to soften me up, then Baron will swan in and lowball an offer."

"Need backup?" Sargent Conrad asks.

"The U.S. Navy will have my back on this one."

"I mean no disrespect and apologize for what I'm about to ask."

Marshall Fields is hedging, the colonel thinks, wondering why women go through such rigmarole before they get to the point.

"Marshall Fields, I would appreciate it if you simply tell us what's on your mind. I'm big enough and ugly enough to take it."

She wrings her hands, takes a deep breath, then looks him in the eye. "Sir, we have noticed a remarkable change in your complexion. Is there anything we should know about your health?"

"I have liver cancer," Colonel Baker says. "Best case, I have eighteen months."

"Worst case?" Hermes asks.

"Three months. That's why Major Hayes is now in charge. I will meet with Baron in two weeks. I'll stay at the Navy base until then."

Colonel Baker looks at his closest allies, his friends: Marshall Fields, Sargent Conrad, Hermes Conrad, Lieutenant Rents and Major Hayes. They say their final goodbyes in silence. "Dismissed."

Chapter Twenty-Eight

An autonomous car drives Colonel Baker to a twenty-story building in downtown Frisco. Baron's own skyscraper. The colonel intends to destroy it. To ensure his infernal plan works, he installed a neuro implant; she will be controlling special pouches that have been fitted inside his body.

The doors open automatically, and the colonel gets through security without incident. He takes the elevator to the 35th floor and smirks when, as expected, the doors open into an attorney's office. A receptionist whisks him into a conference room and brings him a club soda.

"Colonel Baker, are you ready?" the implant asks.

"Yes, let's begin."

The implant releases an anticoagulant followed by a morphine chaser. Soon, a dozen attorneys enter and organize themselves into chairs along the 30-foot-long table. They're all wearing black suits and red ties, apart from one man in a Frisco PD uniform who stands in the corner and scowls.

A pair of gray eyebrows descend into a scowl designed to communicate impatience. The suit wants the colonel to feel powerless. "I can have you arrested right now," he says.

"I'm releasing the toxin and upping your painkillers," the implant says.

Euphoria makes tolerating the attorney's self-important speech easier as he lists dozens of crimes that would justify the colonel's imprisonment.

The colonel smells the toxic chemicals as he breathes them out. Filling this size of room with a lethal dose will only take two minutes. A few hours later, the bumptious attorney, his colleagues and the policeman will die. The longer their exposure, the faster it will kill them. The implant marks off one-minute intervals. When she says, *"Five minutes,"* the lead suit is sweating profusely.

He dabs his forehead with a crisp handkerchief. "Have you heard a word I said?"

"Six minutes."

"Of course. Allow me to summarize. I'm a terrible human being. If I don't do what you say, I go to jail, do not pass go or collect two hundred dollars. Do you have a recording device?"

Gray eyebrows shakes his head.

"You've made a lot of threats, but what is your offer?" Colonel Baker asks.

"I'm not prepared to discuss a deal, not yet. First, you need to understand your situation." His eyelids flutter. He picks up a glass of water, astonished when it falls from his hand.

Colonel Baker leans back into his chair and smiles. "You feel lightheaded because each of you has received a lethal dose of a drug that is clotting your blood. Your heart is struggling to push those sluggish blood cells through your veins. Your brain is starved of oxygen."

The police officer in the corner falls face-first to the floor. A younger man pushes his chair from the table

318

and gets up. He manages to take a few steps before falling.

"In several seconds, you will experience a cascade reaction that will turn all your blood to gelatin."

Lead suit tries to speak, but nothing comes out. His lips turn blue as he points his finger at the colonel. Then, he freezes in place as his blood thickens.

"I call this statue *Arrogance Paused*. Not my best work, I'll admit. All the same, I dedicate it to Hermes the Trickster."

Around the room, blue-faced suits are frozen in place. It could be the pain medication's effect, but Colonel Baker is enjoying himself. He takes out his cell phone and shines a blue light on his suit, degrading the casings containing a virulent strain of black mold. The fungus has been genetically altered and is resistant to chemicals. It will permeate every nook and crevasse. Its spores are highly toxic.

He stands up, hoping the unstable feeling in his legs is caused by the copious amounts of morphine in his system rather than blood clots. He walks around the table and takes the lead suit's keycard and lanyard. He smiles at the receptionist as he leaves the conference room and heads to the elevator.

The keycard allows him to access the penthouse. He takes postage-stamp-sized pieces of fabric the same color as the carpet from his pocket and sprinkles them. Wherever the elevator goes, it will release more black mold spores. The doors open into a luxurious reception guarded by two security men—bulging muscles in cheap suits.

"I have an appointment with Jason Baron."

"No, you don't," a middle-aged woman in a black suit says.

The two security men move closer. "It's time for you to go."

The colonel stalls for time. "Do you know who I am?"

"It doesn't matter if you don't have an appointment."

"Not on the books. But Mr. Baron's attorneys told me to listen to his offer. So, I'm here. If you don't believe me, call the 35th floor." He sits while the receptionist presses buttons on her desk phone.

She freezes while still dialing. It didn't take long.

"Somethings wrong," one guard says but freezes while reaching into his jacket pocket.

The other man falls to the floor. James Baker takes the .22 pistol from the first man's fingers before opening the door to Baron's office.

He's on the phone with his back to the door. "No, if he doesn't take the offer, then cancel the contract," Baron says.

The colonel sits and waits.

"The first batch of chemicals is almost depleted. Should I start the second?"

Colonel Baker shakes his head.

"You want to wait until he faces you?"

He nods.

"I understand. His death will be as slow as possible."

Baron hangs up his desk phone, stands, and looks out the window.

"Nice view," the colonel says, standing up.

Baron turns around quickly and scowls. According to records, Baron is 91 but looks in his mid-forties. He's muscular, but it's all augments. Probably never lifted a weight in his life. "Mr. Baker, how did you get past security?"

"You said you wanted to talk. Let's talk."

"You are a skilled field commander. Kudos. You won the battle, but you lost the war," Baron says. "As you know, much of the vegetation in and around the Sacramento Bayou has a chemical suicide built into the genetic code. I spray a chemical, and the Bayou dies."

The colonel can taste the spiciness of the latest chemical the implant has released. Perfect irony. "So, you're willing to destroy an entire ecosystem and inflict economic harm to Frisco just to get to me?"

Baron is a few inches taller. He steps in close, towering and glowering. The powerplay does not work on the colonel.

The colonel's outward breath makes Baron blink; his left-hand spasms. He staggers back to his desk and presses a button.

"What have you done to me?" he asks between clenched teeth.

"The tetanus bacterium produces a toxin that causes muscle spasms powerful enough to break bones. As you have noticed, the first symptoms tend to happen in the outer extremities, hands, for instance, then jaw, spine."

Baron tries to reach for something in his desk drawer but falls to the floor. His back arches and legs contract. His fists are clenched so tight that his nails make his palms bleed.

Colonel Baker moves his chair and sits next to Baron, whose face is locked in a grimace.

"I'm tired of people like you telling me how to live. Your only source of power is money. It buys the airwaves and bribes officials. You send an army of four thousand against my home, and you think I'm the bad guy."

Baron pants as the spasms relax. If he lives long enough, the next wave is programmed to peak in a few hours, bringing crippling spasms and intense pain.

Two guards stride into the office with their guns drawn. The colonel raises his hands.

"Get him out of here!" Baron yells through clenched teeth.

The toxin is building up, especially within a three-foot radius.

"Get up," the lead security man commands.

The colonel continues to sit, hands raised. "Sorry, bum knee. Can you give an old man a hand?"

The guard grabs the colonel's lapel and pulls. The fabric rips in his hand, releasing a cloud of spores. The man cries out and wipes his eyes.

It isn't long before all three men, the two security guards and Baron, are lying on the floor with arched backs.

"Where was I? That's right, your offer. So, I formally reject your offer and propose a counteroffer. I checked, and you are not insured against terrorist attacks or biological weapons. Right now, your precious building is contaminated with a weaponized black mold. In a few days, it will be unhabitable. Since Baron Enterprises is leveraged to the hilt with your expansion, the loss of the building's income and subsequent clean-up will bankrupt Baron Enterprises."

They are in too much agony to hear. More security personnel walk in but only manage a few steps before coughing from the spores.

"It won't be long now," the implant says.

The colonel wonders whether he should have given her a name. After all, hers will be the last voice he hears.

"I like Anna," she says.

Reverting to military training, the colonel takes the stolen pistol from his jacket pocket and puts a bullet through the head of Baron and everybody else in the room. Then, he sits in Baron's chair.

"Are you ready?" Anna asks.

"Let's do this."

First, the implant floods his bloodstream with painkillers, then releases drugs that will turn his bones to mush within a few hours, and finally, nutrients that nourish the black mold, ensuring its survival. He knows he will be covered in black fuzz within minutes of his death. He'll be a puddle dripping from the chair in a few hours.

He loses feeling in his legs. Someone in a hazmat suit opens the door. Two anonymous white-clad beings stride across the room. The colonel thinks for one moment that they might be angels. Then he notices their rifles. A supreme act of courage and will enables him to rise to his feet. Just before his arms freeze, he gives the men a one-finger salute.

He is answered by a single bullet to the forehead.

Chapter Twenty-Nine

Today is the day we will retake Ceres. Major Gracie Hayes put me in charge of negotiations because I'm the most antagonistic man she knows. It's a gift.

Per my orders, they removed the Stinger missile launcher from the Stryker. It's an eight-wheeled armored vehicle. I kept the mobile gun system but replaced the missile launcher with loudspeakers.

Our special forces, mutants with night vision, retook the harbor without firing a shot. For the past week, we've been moving in equipment. Now, we're ready to take the heavily fortified back gate.

Jason Baron spared no expense. The back gate is fortified with an automatic weapons platform and mobile robot guards. According to the plans Natasha hacked, it's operated by a maximum of nine people who monitor the automated systems and reload ammo during an attack.

The Stryker takes the lead with 60 hardened soldiers behind me. It's a two-mile march up a slight rise, followed by a left turn that leads to the back gate several hundred yards away.

Our soundtrack is *Waterloo* by Abba. I crank up the volume until it sends rumbles through the earth. We stop just outside of weapons range and let the song play.

I sit inside the Stryker and watch the monitors.

"You sure this is going to work?" Major Gracie asks.

I nod. When the song ends, I broadcast my prerecorded advertisement. "Hi, are you feeling alone, abandoned and need to discuss your options. Then call now." It repeats the number three times, and then *Waterloo* plays again. The song gets less than halfway through before my cell phone rings. I cut the music and put the call on speakerphone.

"What do you want?" a male voice on the other end asks.

"I want to bribe you with gold. Are you interested?"

There's a pause. "How much?"

"I understand your installation holds nine guards. So, I have nine one-ounce gold coins."

"There's only three of us," a woman says.

"Shut up!" the male voice answers.

"Okay, my back gate bribery budget is nine ounces of gold. With three people, each gets three ounces. Is that about a year's pay?"

"Eighteen months," the woman's voice says.

"And in exchange for the gold, I only want you to go home and never return. Do we have a deal?"

"There is no way you can take this facility," the male voice says.

"You're right. That's why we plan to surround your facility, just out of weapons range and starve you. How much food do you have?"

Another long pause, then, "We want to see the gold."

"Okay, I'll come over alone. I give you gold, and then you leave. Deal."

"If the gold is real, you have a deal."

A soldier opens the Stryker's back door, and I go down the ramp. Holding a small sack, I head to the back gate. Red lights pepper my shirt from the autonomous weapons. The back door opens, and a bald man with a pot belly frisks me. The facility is brand new and bristling with 50-caliber machine guns and missile launchers. There's a wall of monitors, a break room with lockers and even a vintage-style foosball table. I lay out three stacks of three gold coins on the plastic wood rim. The money disappears into pockets, and before I can say, "Fancy a game," the guards walk out the door, get in their cars, and drive away.

"Darling, I hacked the computer and shut down the system."

I signal for the soldiers to advance. Major Hayes is first in the door. She gets in front of a computer, and her implant worms its way into the system.

While the soldiers dig in, I wait for the front gate to call.

Baron died almost two years ago, but it took another year and a half for the company to declare bankruptcy. Colonel James spread a nasty black mold that condemned the building. The insurance company didn't cover the damages, and because the hazard was biological, it cost more to demolish the skyscraper than to build a new one. So, it still stands sealed and vacant. Baron Enterprises' assets were sold off to creditors. Baron's posh subdivision can't afford enough security to keep us out.

Major Gracie laughs. "The front gate is desperately trying passwords to regain control." She types and chuckles.

Soon, the front gate calls. "Do we get the same deal?"

"How many are left."

"Five people, three coins each, and we walk. But no passwords."

I look at Major Hayes. She nods.

"Deal."

*   *   *

A few more bribes, and by noon, we have retaken Ceres. Next, we must deal with the homeowners. The state gave them deeds to the land that said as long as they pay taxes, they are lawful tenants. Most of the original cinder block and hemp bail homes were demolished, and million-credit-homes were built.

335

In a few hours, the new residents pack as much as they can carry and leave. I'm stuck at the gatehouse while Natasha searches for the right software to open the back doors. I already know what my home will look like. I heard they used it for target practice. It took six months of pounding, but now it's reduced to rubble. Mom says I can stay with them until I rebuild.

It's late afternoon when Natasha hardens the software, and our techs can install a physical switch that can shut down the fiber optic communications.

I take a jog for the first time in over six years. The town is very different. The pavement is wider, and a ten-foot bike path runs from the front gate to the back entrance, about five miles.

I stop outside my house and walk down the driveway. All that remains of my home are piles of concrete and twisted steel. My bank vault front door took a direct hit from an anti-tank missile. Shame. I really liked my door; it was a conversation starter.

In the air are the distant sounds of sporadic weapons fire. I guess not everyone is leaving without a fight.

Chapter Thirty

Luckily, Baron's men were so busy demolishing my house that they overlooked the hidden basement where I stashed my tools and supplies. Rebuilding my home doesn't cost as much as the first remodel. Finally, Natasha understands that no home is bomb-proof.

I expanded the basement and built a concrete house over the top with metal shutters for the windows. The top story is my bedroom with the walk-in closet my alter ego Victoria always dreamed of. The living room and kitchen are downstairs. I replaced my furniture with red cherry wood. The darker colors feel homier.

The rest is made of ultra-modern sawgrass and plastic bails. It connects to one side of the concrete structure and rambles in a U shape around the driveway. The bottom story contains garages and workshops. The top level has five empty rooms. I haven't figured out what to do with them.

The doorbell rings, and Natasha opens the new two-inch nickel steel door.

Mom smiles. She's carrying decorations for Brigette's seventh birthday party. We chat while we set up.

Mom hangs the Happy Birthday sign over the kitchen entrance. "You did a great job homeschooling Brigette."

"I'm not a single-parent, Mom, but thanks. She's not reached the stage where she's happy to sit at a desk and read from a tablet, but she loves paper books she can read outdoors."

"How do you motivate her to read? I remember how hard it was to get you to stay still for five minutes."

I hand Mom a push pin. "Brigette's into dinosaurs, so I get dinosaur books. Last month, it was dragons."

"Is she getting along with her mom?"

"Pam isn't sure what to do with a six-year-old girl that can climb a rope with her arms while carrying her baby brother scissored between her legs."

Mom nods and gets off the step. "You don't have issues with custody?"

When Pam's not out on the water, Brigette sees her mom daily.

I put the ladder away. Then, we step back and admire the decorations.

Mom gives me a long look. "How are you doing?"

I open my mouth to speak, and instead, I weep.

Mom leads me to the couch and lays my head in her lap. I soak her pant leg with my tears while she strokes my hair.

"I don't know why I'm crying," I say.

"I do," Mom says. "You're not a field commander. You're a video journalist. The meanest thing you've ever done was farting on that man's steak."

I chuckle. "I thought he was a local mob boss, not a collegiate athlete."

"It beats me; why you need to use so much profanity when you're being chased?"

I sit up and look at her. She's grinning. I must have inherited my

341

playful streak from her. Mom's ploy is working. I don't feel like curling up in a dark corner any longer.

"Most people aren't long-distance runners. So, I have to encourage them to keep running after me."

"Except for that athlete, he didn't need any encouragement."

I chuckle.

"After the party, why don't you take a vacation and play with your new cameras? We'll help Pam take care of Brigette."

"Yeah, that's a good idea. I need to recharge my batteries."

Chapter Thirty-One

Drucilla's car splutters as she drives through the front gate of Ceres. The three-wheeled mini-diesel started overheating a hundred miles outside Vegas. She's been nursing it with sheer willpower since they entered California. Her son, Rick Junior, is asleep in the back seat.

She drives down the main street, marveling at all the greenery. Ceres is a lot different than the desert of Vegas.

At the Main and Baker Street intersection is a three-story building with the 'Maggie's Bakery and Café' sign. Below in smaller letters, 'Open for

Breakfast and Lunch.' Drew pulls into the parking lot. Before she can turn the key, the car lets out a final cough and dies.

"We're here."

After a quick stretch, she opens the rear door and takes her son by the hand. This trip is a leap of faith. She hired a private detective, but nobody from Denver knows Rick Savage. He said his hometown was Ceres. She hopes that someone here knows Rick and where she might find him.

They enter the café and look around. The dining tables are to her left, booths line both walls, and the counter seats are near the back. A plump black woman walks out from a double-door set leading to the kitchen. She takes one look at Rick and Drucilla, then freezes.

Drew smiles. "Hi, my name is Drucilla, and this is my son, Rick Junior. I'm looking for Rick Savage. Do you know him?"

The woman bursts out laughing, stumbles back to the wall and slides down. She tries to speak but only laughs.

Chapter Thirty-Two

Maggie calls and tells me she made brownies. Chocolate is hard to come by, so this must be a special occasion. I hop in my electric pickup and exit my long drive. It's the last week of June, and my vacation is over.

I needed a few months to myself. I played with cameras and a miniature submarine in the Bayou. I don't like war and telling soldiers what to do any more than I enjoy being told what to do. Maybe that makes me a natural anarchist. I'm in my early thirties and still learning what I don't and do like.

The good thing about children is their uncanny ability to distract me from my brooding. Children give me perspective on what is and isn't important, like going outside and kicking a ball around. Krypto is also good at that. He can tell when I'm thinking about the war. So, he brings me a ball, and we play fetch. Usually, I end up chasing Krypto around the yard.

I turn right and head down Main Street. Krypto knows where we're going. I keep my speed at 15mph, and he runs along the bike path. He frequently stops for a sniff but always manages to catch up.

I wait for someone to pull out and take their spot. The parking lot is unusually busy for mid-afternoon; Maggie's is normally quiet after lunch. Krypto jumps into the truck bed to sleep until it's time to leave.

I walk inside. The booths are full, and there's only one seat left at the counter. I sit down, and the woman to my right puts her hand on mine. I look over, and it's Drucilla.

"Hey, you're out of context," I say and hug her. "What are you doing here?"

Drew gets up and leads me by the hand. "I have someone to show you."

We walk to a back booth and sit beside a young boy who looks a lot like me and my father. He's got the Conrad forehead with two bumps that look like small horns. Mom and Daniel are there, too. Mom's looking very pleased with herself.

"What's your name?" I ask.

"Rick, Rick Junior."

I smile. "Well, my name's Hermes, so you're not a junior, just Rick."

Rick puts his hand on his forehead. "Thank God. Can you imagine being a hundred years old?" Rick hunches over. "Junior, I need you to go to the pharmacy and pick up some more ointment for my scabies."

We laugh at his impression, and then I check my virtual watch. "You want to meet your sister? There's a soccer game starting in fifteen minutes. You can play if you want."

Rick ducks under the table and runs toward the exit.

Drew laughs. "I guess that's a yes. I'm sorry. It's been a long drive, and I'm a little overwhelmed."

My mom is as smooth as molasses and seizes her opportunity. "Why don't you two have some couple-time while we get acquainted with our grandson."

Drew and I get in the truck. Krypto sticks his head through the back window and gives Drew a sniff and lick. She sniffs him back and licks his nose. Krypto pulls his head back, gives a puzzled look and then attacks Drew with his tongue. Drew retaliates, but Krypto is the clear winner. I open a compartment between the seats and give Drew a long-sleeved sweatshirt.

She wipes her face. "I want to get a few things off my chest."

"Okay."

"I fought with my parents and left home on bad terms. I rejected their values, the bad ones and the good ones. I used my abilities to manipulate people, and I regret it. Mr. Big took me in and helped me sort through my stuff. I'm grateful."

I nod. "Trolls are good people. And I've also used my abilities in ways that I regret. Full disclosure: I'm a sociopath. This is a fancy way of saying I like stealing; I am impulsive, and I seduce women using fake names. Six years of war has tempered my character."

"Yeah, my son, our son, has tested me. I checked his internet history. Do you know what site Rick visits the most?" She doesn't wait for me to answer. "Encyclopedia, Rick is up to the Ps."

"I went through my vacuuming up information stage. We'll get him a printed copy. Better for his eyes."

She takes a deep breath and lets it out. "I thought I could raise Rick alone, but he is more than a handful. So, I came to Ceres to find Rick Savage. The townspeople take one look at my son and declare him a Conrad. I'd like to think that makes us part of a tribe."

I smile. "It's a small town, that's for sure."

We pull into a parking lot. Kids are playing soccer in the distance. I spot my son's bluish-black hair.

"Before we get out, I have a checklist. There are two more items."

"Okay."

"I'm twenty-seven-and-a-half years old, the bio clock is ticking, and I want a girl."

I smile. "Do you mind if we settle in and get to know each other before we add another character to the play."

Drew closes her eyes and pauses for a moment. "I understand what you're saying intellectually and agree with you. However, I tend to spontaneously ovulate when I orgasm. It's getting worse the older I get. I have zero self-control. So, if you don't want more kids, you're in charge of birth control."

Natasha is a horn dog, and I'm impulsive by nature. I throw my head back and laugh, then lean in and kiss her lightly. "That's something we have in common, zero self-control."

She whispers in my ear. "One last thing. If you agree, I'm all yours. I want to raise chickens."

I sit back. "What type, meat, eggs or for show?"

"What are Silkies?"

"That's a show chicken. There are a few dozen people who raise chickens in Ceres. They can give you pointers while I build a coop."

"Okay, that's my list. Do you have any deal breakers in a relationship?"

"Are you vegetarian?"

"No."

"Then you meet my exacting standards."

We hold hands as we walk to the soccer field. Mom and Dad are standing next to Pam and Jessie. Their three-year-old son is on Jessie's shoulders. We join them and watch our children play. I was always apprehensive about having a family. Unfortunately, the problems between purebloods and mutants are not going away. Corporations will always try to squeeze as much profit as possible. And human beings will always have to push back against their bullying. But you can't put your life on hold because the world isn't perfect.

The game ends, and parents collect their children.

Everyone looks at me with big grins, so I say, "Let's have a barbeque at my—our home."

We head back to our trucks, drive past Maggie's, and after another mile, left into my driveway.

Drew and Rick look at my wrap-around hemp bail house that ends in a two-story concrete structure with a three-story tower. I suddenly realize what the spare rooms are for—family.

"Is that an observatory?" Rick asks.

"No, that's a megawatt laser to shoot down drones and missiles. Your father has enemies. That means you have enemies. You'll need to learn self-defense and can't leave town without an armed escort."

He laughs, and I smile. Let him think I'm joking. He can learn about the bad stuff later.

The thick steel door opens.

I look at Drew, pull her close, and whisper. "Is that a deal breaker?"

Drew smiles. "No. I vetted everyone who did business with Mr. Big, so I always had an escort. Ceres is just like Las Vegas, with trees."

"Okay, then, let's eat."

Krypto runs inside first, with Rick following.

Books by Wade Coleman

Fiction

Shadow Dragon
Shadow Dragon 2- Bayou Days
Citizen D

Non Fiction

Sepher Sapphires Volume 1 and 2
The Astrology Workbook
The Magic of the Planets
The Zodiac of Dendara Egypt
The Magical Path